新編
成人英語課程
ENGLISH COURSE
for Adults

2

New Edition

舒盛宗編著

萬里機構 • 萬里書店出版

新編成人英語課程 (2)

編著
舒盛宗

責任編輯
阿柿　Eva Lam

封面設計
任霜兒

版面設計
何秋雲

出版者
萬里機構出版有限公司
香港鰂魚涌英皇道1065號東達中心1305室
電話：2564 7511
傳真：2565 5539
電郵：info@wanlibk.com
網址：http://www.wanlibk.com
http://www.facebook.com/wanlibk

發行者
香港聯合書刊物流有限公司
香港新界大埔汀麗路36號
中華商務印刷大廈3字樓
電話：2150 2100
傳真：2407 3062
電郵：info@suplogistics.com.hk

承印者
中華商務彩色印刷有限公司

出版日期
二零一三年七月第一次印刷
二零一九年四月第二次印刷

Published in Hong Kong.
ISBN 978-962-14-4842-2

萬里機構

萬里 Facebook

編輯例言

這套課本顧名思義，是專為成年人學英語而編寫的。

成年人學習外語，理解力較強，記憶力則較差；由於平日事務紛紜，學習時間不夠充裕。因此，編寫成年人的英語課本，與學校課本不同。內容要精簡，要切合成年人的生活，要基礎與應用並重。

這套課本全套共有兩冊，各冊均附QR code記錄讀音。第二冊著重應用，第一部份為十二類常用語句，易學易用。第二部份為會話，每個情景配以數組對話，共有常見情景二十八個。

為了克服成年人記憶力差、發音生硬的弱點，讀者可跟着QR code內記載的讀音，反覆練習，直至大部分句子能記在腦中，信口說出，清楚流暢。這是學習講英語（Spoken English）最有效的方法。

所有課文都以英文、中文對照形式編排，便於自學。

讀者對每一課都必須學至完全能夠聽得懂、讀得熟，才學習下一課，這樣穩紮穩打，就能收到實效。

目錄

PART 01

General Expressions and Phrases

常用語句

本課目標

學用十二組常用語句，以單句發話和回應，邁出英語會話第一步。

1. Greeting 打招呼

Asking after somebody 向人問候

Formal 正式

1011.mp3

Good morning.	早晨（早上）。
Good afternoon.	午安（下午）。
Good evening.	晚安（傍晚）。
Good night.	晚安（夜晚）。

Somebody you first meet 初次見面的人

1012.mp3

How do you do?	你好。

Somebody you've known already 舊相識

1013.mp3

How are you?	你好嗎？
How are you doing?	你近況如何？

Informal 非正式

1014.mp3

How are things (with you)?	你好嗎？
How's it going?	日子過得怎樣？
How's everything?	一切安好？
How's life?	生活過得好嗎？
How's things?	近來怎樣？

Fancy seeing you her.	想不到在這裏遇見你。
Haven't run into you for ages.	真是好久不見。
Long time no see!	好久不見。
It's been a long time.	好久不見。
What a coincidence!	真巧合！
Good to see you!	見到你真高興。
Small world, isn't it?	世界真細小，又跟你踫面了。
What a surprise!	沒想到會見到你。
What brings you here today?	今天什麼風把你吹來？

Responding to people's greeting 回應別人的招呼

Formal 正式

1015.mp3

I'm fine, thank you.	很好，謝謝你。
Pretty good, thank you.	很好，謝謝你。
Quite well, thank you.	很好，謝謝你。
I'm very well indeed, thank you.	我真的很好，謝謝你。
Wonderful. Things couldn't be better.	好得不得了。
Not very good, thank you.	不太好，謝謝你。

Informal 非正式

1016.mp3

Just fine.	很好。
Fine, thanks.	很好，謝謝你。
Great, and you?	很好，你呢？
I'm just great.	我過得很好。
Can't complain	還過得去。
No complaints.	沒什麼可抱怨。
Not too bad, thanks.	不太差，謝謝你。
The usual rounds.	還是老樣子。
So-so, thanks.	馬馬虎虎，謝謝你。

口語貼士：縮寫

會話裏常常都應用縮寫形式。以下為常見例子：

I have=I've	was not=wasn't	cannot=can't
you have=you've	were not=weren't	could not=couldn't
they have=they've	do not=don't	shall not=shan't
I shall/will=I'll	does not=doesn't	should not=shouldn't
you shall/will=you'll	did not=didn't	will not=won't
she shall/will=she'll	has not=hasn't	would not=wouldn't
I had, I would=I'd	have not=haven't	must not=mustn't
we had, we would=we'd	had not=hadn't	
you had, you would=you'd		

2. Starting a conversation 談話開場白

傳統的英國人大多數都會用「天氣狀況」來作與人談話的開場白，無論對象是熟朋友或陌生人，同樣適用。

PART 01

1021.mp3

Cold weather, isn't it?	天氣很冷，不是嗎？
Dreadful weather, don't you think?	這天氣真令人討厭，你說不是嗎？
It's freezing, isn't?	冷極了，不是嗎？
Horrible weather we're having.	天氣糟透了。
Nice (Wonderful) day, isn't it?	天氣真好，不是嗎？

Formal 正式

1022.mp3

Excuse me, aren't you Peter Chan?	對不起，你不是陳彼德嗎？
Do excuse me, please, but are you Peter Chan?	請見諒，你是否陳彼德？
Please pardon me for asking, but aren't you Mr. Peter Chan?	請原諒我問一下，你不是陳彼德先生嗎？
I hope you don't mind my asking, but haven't we met somewhere before?	希望你不介意我發問，我們是不是以前在什麼地方見過嗎？
Please forgive me for asking, but do you mind if I open the window?	請原諒我發問，你介意我開窗嗎？

Informal 非正式

1023.mp3

Hello!	你好！
Say, don't I know you from somewhere?	喂！我們是不是在某地見過面？
Hi! You're Mr. Peter Chan, then?	你好！你是陳彼德先生嗎？
Sorry, but can I have a look at the newspaper?	對不起，我可以看看這份報紙嗎？

3. Introduction 介紹

Self-introduction 自我介紹

Formal 正式

1031.mp3

Allow me to introduce myself: Paul Chan, a teacher from Hong Kong.	請容我自我介紹：陳保羅，來自香港的老師。
Excuse me. I don't believe we've met before, I'm Sam Leung.	對不起。我相信我們還沒有見過面。我是梁森美。
How do you do? My name is Charles White.	你好。我的名字叫韋查爾斯。
May I introduce myself: Donald Lee.	請允許我自我介紹：李當奴。
Please let me introduce myself: David Tam.	請讓我自我介紹：譚大偉。

Informal 非正式

1032.mp3

Hello! I'm Tony Chan.	你好！我是陳東尼。
Hi! I'm Harry Chow.	你好！我是周夏利。

Responding to an introduction 應答他人介紹

Formal 正式

1033.mp3

How do you do?	你好！
I'm very (happy/glad/delighted) to meet you.	我很高興認識你。
I'm very pleased to make your acquaintance.	我很高興認識你。
It's a pleasure to meet you.	很榮幸認識你。

Informal 非正式

1034.mp3

Hi!	你好！
Oh, hello!	噢，你好！
Glad to meet you.	很高興認識你。
Nice meeting you.	很高興認識你。
Nice to meet you.	很高興認識你。

4. Saying good-bye 告辭

Formal 正式

1041.mp3

Good-bye. Nice seeing you.	再見，很高興見到你。
Good-bye then, and all the very best.	再見，祝萬事如意。
Be in touch.	保持聯絡。
Keep in touch.	保持聯絡。
Remember to drop me a line.	記住給我寫信。
Remember to look me up if you are ever here.	如你再來此地，記得來探我。

Informal 非正式

1042.mp3

Cheerio!	再見！
See you.	再見！(短暫離開)
See you around!	回頭見！
See you later!	稍後再見！
See you soon!	回頭見！
So long!	再見！
Adieu!	再見！(古英語)
Take care. Bye.	保重，再見。

5. Compliment 稱讚

Formal 正式

1051.mp3

May I say how elegant you look with this necklace?	我想説你戴着這項鏈真高貴。
My compliments on your memory.	我佩服你的記憶力。
May I say how charming you look?	我想説你很迷人。
You English is excellent.	你的英語非常好。
How lucky you are!	你真幸運！
That's a very nice hair-style you're wearing.	你的髮型很美。
You look really wonderful in this dress.	你穿這裙子真是好看極了。
Your necklace goes really well with your skin.	你的項鏈與你的膚色很相襯。

Informal 非正式

1052.mp3

Lucky you!	你真幸運！
You look great!	你漂亮極了！
You're looking good!	你很好看！
You look very smart.	你很英俊。
Wonderful!	漂亮極了！
What a terrific watch you have!	你的手錶漂亮極了！
What a nice hat!	這頂帽子真漂亮。

Responding to Compliments 對稱讚的回答

Formal 正式

1053.mp3

How very kind of you to say so.	非常感謝你這麼説。
It's very good of you to say so.	謝謝你這麼説。
Oh, it's nothing special actually.	噢，實際上沒什麼特別的。
Thank you. I'm very glad you think so.	謝謝你。我很高興你這麼想。
Thank you. I'll take it as compliment.	謝謝你。我當是你真心的稱讚了。

Informal 非正式

1054.mp3

Oh, I'm flattered.	過獎了。
Oh, really?	噢，真的嗎？
Oh, not really.	噢，不會吧。
Oh, nothing to it actually.	噢，實際上沒什麼。
Oh, thanks.	噢，謝謝。

6. Wishes and congratulations 祝福與恭賀

General Wishes 一般祝福

1061.mp3

Bless you!	祝福你！（當友人打噴嚏時說這話）
Good Luck.	祝你好運！
Happy New Year!	新年快樂！
Merry Christmas!	聖誕快樂！
Happy birthday to you!	祝你生日快樂！
Congratulations.	恭喜！
All the best!	祝你萬事如意。
The best of luck.	祝你好運！

Formal 正式

1062.mp3

Please remember me to your parents.	請代我向你的父母問候。
Please give my best wishes to your parents.	請向你的父母致意。
Let's toast the health of Mr. Li.	讓我們乾杯，祝李先生身體健康。
I'd like to propose a toast to bride and groom.	我提議為新郎新娘乾杯。
Allow me to express my heartiest congratulations.	請允許我對你表示最衷心的祝賀。
Please accept my sincere congratulations.	請接受我最衷心的祝賀。

Informal 非正式

1063.mp3

Fantastic!	太精采了！
Bravo!	精采極了！
Well done!	做得好！

Making Good Wishes to somebody's vacation 為友人遠遊祝福

Formal 正式

1064.mp3

I wish you a pleasant journey.	祝你旅途愉快！
I hope you enjoy your visit to New York.	希望你會享受到紐約的旅程。
I hope you have a good time.	祝你旅途愉快！

Informal 非正式

1065.mp3

Nice Trip!	一路順風！
Bon voyage!	旅途愉快！(法語)
Enjoy your flight!	飛行愉快！
Happy journey!	旅途愉快！
Have a good time!	祝你旅途愉快！
Have fun.	玩得開心點。

口語貼士：命令語氣

❶ 動詞有命令語氣（imperative mood），用於表示一個命令、勸諫或要求：

1066.mp3

Stand up.	站起來。
Be a good boy!	做一個好孩子。
Give me a cup of coffee, please.	請給我一杯咖啡。

❷ 命令語氣一律用不帶to的動詞不定式，轉為否定句時，在句首加上do not（don't）：

1067.mp3

Don't stop!	不要停下來！
Don't be noisy!	不要吵鬧！

❸ 命令語氣一般用於第二人稱，例如Stand up應為You stand up，不過you字被省略掉罷了。用於第一和第三人稱時要用let。例如：

1068.mp3

Let me try.	讓我試試看。
Let us（Let's）go!	讓我們走吧！
Let him do it.	讓他做吧。

❹ Let us通常縮寫為Let's.

7. Thanks 答謝

General response to show thanks 一般情況表示謝意

🎧 1071.mp3

Thank you.	謝謝你。
Thank you for your kindness.	謝謝你的好意。
Thank you very much.	非常感謝。
Thanks a lot.	多謝。
Thanks a million.	非常感謝。
Many thanks.	謝謝。

Responding to Wishes 回應別人對你的祝福

🎧 1072.mp3

How very kind of you to say so.	非常感謝你這麼說。
It's very good of you to say so.	謝謝你這樣說。
Thank you. And I wish you the same!	謝謝你，我也同樣祝福你！
Thanks. The same to you!	謝謝你，你也一樣！
It's most thoughtful of you.	你想得真周到。

Responding to compliments 回應別人對你的讚賞

1073.mp3

How very kind of you to say so.	非常感謝你這麼説。
It's very good of you to say so.	謝謝你這樣説。
Oh! I'm flattered.	過獎了。
Oh, you flatter me.	你過獎了。

Responding to thanks 回應別人對你的答謝

1074.mp3

It's a pleasure.	我很樂意。
My pleasure.	我很樂意。
Pleasure is mine.	我很樂意。
Not at all.	別客氣。
No trouble at all.	沒什麼。
Please don't mention it.	不用客氣。
You are welcome.	不用客氣。

8. Apologies 道歉

PART 01

Formal 正式

1081.mp3

I can't tell you how sorry I am.	我實在難以表達我的歉意。
I do apologize for that.	我確實要為此向你道歉。
I do beg your pardon.	請你見諒。
I hope you will excuse me.	我希望你能原諒我。
I must apologize.	我必須要道歉。
I'm extremely sorry.	我非常抱歉。
I'm awfully sorry.	非常抱歉。
I'm terribly sorry about that.	我對此非常抱歉。
I just don't know what to say.	我不知該説什麼才好。
Please forgive me. I really didn't mean that.	請原諒。我實在沒有那個意思。
It was most careless of me.	這是我的疏忽。
It was really quite unintentional.	我不是故意的。
I'm afraid I've brought you too much trouble.	抱歉給你帶來許多麻煩。

Informal 非正式

1082.mp3

I'm sorry.	對不起。
Excuse me!	對不起或請原諒。
Pardon me.	對不起或請原諒。
Oh, it's my fault.	哦，是我不好。
Oh, how silly am I!	哦，我真笨。

Sorry!	對不起。
Sorry about that!	那件事很對不起。
I really feel bad about that.	我實在為此感到不安。
A thousand pardons!	萬分抱歉。

Responding to somebody's apologies 回應別人的道歉

Formal 正式

1083.mp3

Please don't blame yourself.	不要怪責自己。
Please don't worry.	請別在意。
It's really not necessary.	這實在沒有必要。
Never mind. It doesn't matter at all.	實在沒有什麼要緊的。
Don't let it worry you.	不要為此不安。

Informal 非正式

1084.mp3

Forget it.	別放在心上。
It's OK.	沒問題。
No problem.	沒問題。
No harm!	不礙事。
Not to worry.	別擔心。
That's all right.	沒有關係。
Please don't feel bad about it.	請不要為此感到不快。

9. Requests 請求

Asking for Permission 請求許可

PART 01

Formal 正式

1091.mp3

Do I have your permission?	你允許我嗎？
Will you do me a favour?	可以幫忙嗎？
Am I allowed to sit here?	可以坐在這裏嗎？
May I come in?	可以進來嗎？
Could I ask you a question?	可以問你一個問題嗎？
Would you mind if I smoke here?	你不介意我在這兒抽煙嗎？
Would you mind my smoking here?	你不介意我在這兒抽煙嗎？
Would you mind closing the window (for me)?	你不介意為我關上那窗子吧？
Do you have any objection if I take a day off?	我想休假一天，你反對嗎？
I wonder whether (if) I could possibly take it away?	我可否把它拿走。

Informal 非正式

1092.mp3

Please help me.	請幫個忙。
All right?	行嗎？
Any chance?	有可能嗎？
Mind if I smoke?	你不介意我抽煙吧？
Let me have that, would you?	給我這個好嗎？
Have I got the go-ahead?	行嗎？

Have I got the go-ahead to speak to the boss?	我可以跟老闆說嗎？
Can I have the OK?	行嗎？
OK to lend me your mobile?	借你的手電我用行嗎？
Is there any way I could use your laptop?	能不能借你的手提電腦給我用？

Giving somebody permission 給人許可

Formal 正式

1093.mp3

I can see no objection.	我想沒什麼不可以的。
I can't see any reason why you shouldn't do that.	你要去做也沒什麼不可以的。
I don't find any objection.	我看不出有什麼不可以的。
That seems perfectly acceptable.	這似乎是完全可接受的。
Yes, indeed.	是的，真的可以。
You may smoke, if you like.	你想的話，就抽（煙）吧！

Informal 非正式

1094.mp3

All right.	行。
Anything goes!	隨你怎樣也行！
Feel free!	隨便你。
Suit yourself.	隨便你。
Fine.	好的。
Go Ahead!	去走吧。

By all means.	當然可以。
Yes, certainly.	當然可以。
It's OK!	當然可以。
Sure.	當然可以。
To be sure!	當然可以。
No reason why not.	沒什麼不可以的。

Refusing to give somebody permission 拒絕給人許可

Formal 正式

1095.mp3

I'm afraid I can't give you permission to open the door.	恐怕我不能允許你打開這門。
I'm afraid I can't permit that.	恐怕我不能允許此事。
I'm sorry, but that's not possible.	對不起，但這是不可能的。
I'm sorry. That's not allowed.	對不起，這是允許的。
I'm afraid it's against the regulations to do that.	這麼做恐怕是違反規定的。

Informal 非正式

1096.mp3

No, you can't.	你不能。
No way, I'm afraid.	恐怕不行。
Of course not.	當然不可以。
Impossible.	對不可能。
Out of the question, I'm afraid.	恐怕不可能。

Sorry, no way.	對不起，不可以。
I don't think so.	我不同意。

口語貼士：如何令語氣變得婉轉？

❶ 英語的常用語句面，常常碰到could, should, would等字。could, should, would為can, shall, will的過去式，這些過去式常用來表示現在的動作，與現在式的語氣不同。例如could可以代替can，但語氣較為婉轉：

Could you persuade him to come back?	你能説服他回來嗎？
I couldn't possibly finish the work on time.	我實在不能依時完成工作。

❷ should用於現在時態，作「應當」解：

You should listen to his advice.	你應該聽他的話。
He should be more careful.	他應該小心點。

❸ should又可用於表示「期望」或「可能」：

She should be there by now.	她現在可能到了。
The book should be on the bookshelf.	那本書可能在書架上。

❹ would不論是表達説話人本身的意志或向對方提出請求，均較will為婉轉、客氣：

Would you mind closing the door for me?	請你替我把門關上好嗎？
Would you like a drink?	你要喝點東西嗎？

10. Suggestions 提議

Formal 正式

1101.mp3

I wonder whether you'd like to go hiking this weekend?	不知道這周末你是否想去遠足？
Would you like to have lunch at this Japanese restaurant?	你想在這日本餐廳吃午飯嗎？
May I suggest painting this room in pink?	我可不可以建議在這房間塗上粉紅色油漆？
Would you care to have a drink with me?	你願意與我喝一杯嗎？

Informal 非正式

1102.mp3

Fancy a drink?	想喝一杯嗎？
Feel like a game of tennis?	想打場網球嗎？
How about going for a movie tonight?	今晚不如去看齣電影吧。
Let's go for a walk.	出外逛逛街吧。
What about having our car washed?	把我們的車洗乾淨吧。
Why don't we go fishing this weekend?	周末去釣魚怎麼樣？
Would you like some more?	要多一點嗎？
I've got a really good idea.	我有一個好主意。

Giving positive responses 贊成提議

Formal 正式

1103.mp3

I think that's an excellent proposal (idea)!	我認為這是個極佳建議。
I think your suggestion is acceptable.	我認為你的建議可以接受。
That sounds like a good idea.	聽起來似乎是個好主意。

Informal 非正式

1104.mp3

That's a good idea.	真是好主意。
Not a bad idea.	主意不錯。
It's a lovely idea.	主意極佳。
That'll be just fine.	主意很好。
I'd love to.	好的。
Good enough.	好的。
Will do.	好的。
OK, that's fine.	這好極了。
Sounds good to me.	主意不錯。
That's great.	好極了。
That's my cup of tea.	這正合我的胃口。

Giving negative responses 拒絕提議

Formal 正式

1105.mp3

I regret to say I can't accept your suggestion.	我很抱歉我不能接納你的提議。
I'm afraid your proposal is not acceptable.	我恐怕你的提議不被接受。
I must say I find it unacceptable.	我得說我覺得這是不能接受的。
That's not a very good idea.	這個主意不太好。

Informal 非正式

1106.mp3

Impossible.	不可能。
No way.	不行。
No.	不行。
Can't be done.	不行。
Surely not!	怎麼能這樣。

11. Questions 問句

1111.mp3

How?	怎樣？
How much?	多少錢？
How many?	多少？
How long?	多長？
How far?	多遠？
How often?	多久？
How old are you?	你幾歲？
How much is it?	這個多少錢？
What's this?	這是什麼？
What's your name?	你叫什麼名字？
What's the matter?	什麼事兒啊？
What happened?	發生了什麼事情？
What's the date today?	今天幾號？
What day is it today?	今天星期幾？
What time is it?	幾點鐘？
What can I do for you?	有什麼我可以幫忙？

1112.mp3

Why?	為什麼？
Why are you so late?	你為什麼遲到？
Why not?	為什麼不能？
Why so?	為什麼會這樣的？

Where are you going?	你上哪兒去？
Where does he live?	他住在什麼地方？
Where is she?	她在哪兒？
When will he come back?	他什麼時候回來？
When will you leave?	你什麼時候離開？
Do you like it?	你喜歡這個嗎？
Do you understand?	你明白嗎？
Did you tell him?	你告訴他了嗎？
Did he go?	他有沒有去？
Did he understand the question?	他明白了問題沒有？
Did she come?	她有沒有來？

口語貼士：如何問時間、地點、原因、狀態？

When, Where, Why, How 等為疑問副詞（interrogative adverbs），用以修飾問句中的動詞，表示時間、地點、原因、狀態。例如：

1113.mp3

When will you come back?	你何時回來？
I'll come back in a few weeks.	我幾個星期後回來。
Where are you going?	你上哪兒去？
I'm going to the Peak.	我上山頂去。
Why did you punish him?	你為甚麼責罰他？
I punished him because he cheated during the examination.	他考試作弊，所以我責罰他。

How does he sing?	他唱歌唱得怎麼樣？
He sings beautifully.	他唱得十分好。
How tall is that building?	那座大廈有多高？
It's fifty-two stories high.	這座大廈有五十二層高。

🎧 1114.mp3

Who?	誰？
Whom?	誰？
Who's speaking?	是誰呀？
Who's that man?	那個男人是誰？
Who's your mother?	誰是你的母親？
Who's that girl?	那個女孩子是誰？
Which?	哪一個？
Which bus must I take?	我該乘哪一路線的公共汽車？
Which one do you want?	你要哪一個呢？
Which is better?	哪一個比較好？
Which is the best?	哪一個最好？
Which is yours?	哪一個是你的？
Which way should I go?	我該走哪一條路？
Which is longer?	哪一個比較長？
Which is the longest?	哪一個最長？

口語貼士：如何問人或物？

Who, Whom, Whose, What, Which 等為疑問代名詞（interrogative pronouns），代表問句中要問及的人或物：

1115.mp3

Who is he?	他是誰？
He is Mr. Wong.	他是王先生。
Whom did you meet on the street?	你在街上遇見了誰？
I met my classmate on the street.	我在街上遇見了我的同學。
Whose umbrella is this?	這把雨傘是誰的？
It's mine.	是我的。
What did you buy?	你買了甚麼東西？
I bought several books.	我買了幾本書。
Which book do you want?	你要哪本書？
I want the white one.	我要那本白色的。
Which is your sister?	哪一位是你的妹妹（姊姊）？
The tallest girl is my sister.	那個長得最高的女子是我的妹妹（姊姊）。

12. Excalmations 感嘆句

1121.mp3

That's splendid!	那好極了！
How nice!	多好！
I'm so glad!	我很高興！
How lucky!	多幸運！
How fortunate!	多好運！
How happy I am!	我多麼開心！
I had a very good time!	我過了段很快樂的時光！
Splendid!	好極了！
Excellent!	真妙！
Wonderful!	真好！
Oh, my!	啊，我的天！
Good heavens!	我的天！
Whata pity!	真可惜！
Oh, dear me!	啊，天呀！
Alas!	哎呀！

PART 02

CONVERSATION

會話

本課目標

學會簡短英語對話，應付各類情景。另配生詞表，豐富詞彙。英語會話實戰入門。

1. Time and date 時間、日期

2011.mp3

A: Excuse me. What time is it now?	對不起，請問現在幾點鐘？
B: It's exactly three o'clock❶.	剛好三點鐘。
A: My watch is five minutes slow❷.	我的錶慢了五分鐘。
B: Well, yes. I set my watch by the radio this morning. So I'm sure it's right.	是的。今天早上我跟電台對準了錶。所以我相信這是準確的時間。

2012.mp3

A: What time is it by your watch?	你的錶幾點鐘了？
B: It's eleven fifteen (or a quarter past eleven).	十一點十五分。
A: Is it? My watch says eleven twenty.	真的嗎？我的錶已經十一點二十分了。
B: Your watch is five minutes fast.	你的錶快了五分鐘。

2013.mp3

A: What's the time now?	現在幾點鐘？
B: It's ten minutes to four.	差十分鐘四點了。
A: I must go now.	我現在得走了。
B: Why?	為甚麼？
A: I have to meet Mary at half past four.	我跟瑪麗約定了四點半見面。

2014.mp3

A: When will you go to the park?	你甚麼時候到公園去？
B: Tomorrow, about eight in the morning.	明天早上八點鐘。
A: Then you won't go to the library, will you?	那麼你不到圖書館去了，是嗎？
B: Yes, I'll go there at four in the afternoon.	不是，我下午四點鐘到那裏去。
A: Can you tell me what day it is today❸?	你可以告訴我今天是甚麼日子嗎？
B: It's July the 10th.	七月十號。
A: No, I mean what day of the week is it?	不是這個。我想知道今天是星期幾。
B: Oh, I see. It's Monday.	哦，我明白了。今天是星期一。

2015.mp3

A: What's the date today?	今天幾號？
B: Today is the first of April❹.	今天是四月一號。
A: When will you leave Hong Kong?	你甚麼時候離開香港？
B: Tomorrow afternoon.	明天下午。

文法及用法説明

❶ 要表示時間，可以用下面的方法。

8:00（讀作eight o'clock）
8:10（讀作eight-ten或ten minutes past eight）
8:15（讀作eight-fifteen或a quarter past eight）
8:30（讀作eight-thirty或half past eight）
8:35（讀作eight-thirty-five或twenty-five minutes to nine）
8:45（讀作eight-forty-five或a quarter to nine）
記着在每點鐘的前三十分用...minutes past...，過了三十分鐘，應説...minutes to...。美國的習慣，是用after來代替past，用before代替to。要表示上午或下午，可以用以下的方法： 8:00a.m.（上午八時）讀作eight a.m.，8:00p.m.（下午八時）讀作eight p.m.。在口語，我們也可以説： at eight in the morning（早上八時），at twelve noon（正午十二時），at two in the afternoon（下午二時），at eight in the evening(晚上八時)，at twelve midnight(午夜十二時)。

❷ 如果時鐘或手錶走快了，我們可以説...minute fast，走慢了則説...minute slow。

❸ 詢問日期，要用以下的問句： What date is it today? 或What day of the month is it? 詢問今天是星期幾，要這樣説： What day is it today? 或What day of the week is it?

❹ 要表示日期，美國式的寫法是April 1, 1999.（一九九九年四月一日，讀作April the first, nineteen ninety-nine），英國式的寫法是1st April, 1999.（讀作the first of April, nineteen ninety-nine）。注意表示日子要用序數詞first, second, third...，而不是用數詞one, two, three...。年份的讀法，要分開作兩個數字來讀，例如1900年nineteen hundred、1902年nineteen hundred and two、1915年nineteen fifteen、1950年nineteen fifty。

2000年是 Year Two Thousand、2001年 two thousand and one、2013年就是two thousand and thirteen，如此類推：

year two thousand	2000
year two thousand and one	2001
year two thousand and two	2002
year two thousand and three	2003
year two thousand and four	2004
year two thousand and five	2005
year two thousand and six	2006
year two thousand and seven	2007
year two thousand and eight	2008
year two thousand and nine	2009
year two thousand and ten	2010
year two thousand and eleven	2011
year two thousand and twelve	2012
year two thousand and thirteen	2013
year two thousand and fourteen	2014

Vocabulary 生詞

2016.mp3

week (seven days)	**星期（七天）**
week day (s)	星期一至星期五 （上班與上學的日子）
Sunday	星期日
Monday	星期一
Tuesday	星期二
Wednesday	星期三
Thursday	星期四
Friday	星期五
Saturday	星期六
weekend	星期六與星期日、周末 （通常不用上班與上學的日子）
yesterday	昨天
today	今天
tomorrow	明天
last week	上星期
next week	下星期

2017.mp3

month(s)	**月份**
January	一月

February	二月
March	三月
April	四月
May	五月
June	六月
July	七月
August	八月
September	九月
October	十月
November	十一月
December	十二月
last month	上月
next month	下月

2018.mp3

day		**日期**
first	1st	一日
second	2nd	二日
third	3rd	三日
fourth	4th	四日
fifth	5th	五日
sixth	6th	六日

seventh	7th	七日
eighth	8th	八日
ninth	9th	九日
tenth	10th	十日
eleventh	11th	十一日
twelfth	12th	十二日
thirteenth	13th	十三日
fourteenth	14th	十四日
fifteenth	15th	十五日
sixteenth	16th	十六日
seventeenth	17th	十七日
eighteenth	18th	十八日
nineteenth	19th	十九日
twentieth	20th	二十日
twenty-first	21st	二十一日
twenty-second	22nd	二十二日
twenty-third	23rd	二十三日
twenty-fourth	24th	二十四日
twenty-fifth	25th	二十五日
twenty-sixth	26th	二十六日

twenty-seventh	27th	二十七日
twenty-eighth	28th	二十八日
twenty-ninth	29th	二十九日
thirtieth	30th	三十日
thirty-first	31st	三十一日

calendar 月曆

Exercise 練習

2019.mp3

Answer the following questions. 請回答下列問題。

1. What time is it now?（three o'clock）
2. What's your name?（Li）
3. What day is it today?（Monday）
4. What day of the week is it today?（Friday）
5. What's the date today?（1st of April）

Answers 答案

1. It's three o'clock.
2. My name's Li.
3. It's Monday.
4. It's Friday.
5. It's first of April.

2. The weather 天氣

2021.mp3

A: Nice and warm today, isn't it?	今天的天氣很暖和，對嗎？
B: It certainly is.	對的。
A: I like this kind of weather.	我喜歡這種天氣。
B: I guess everybody does.	我相信每一個人都會喜歡的。

2022.mp3

A: Where are you going?	你上哪兒去？
B: To John's house.	到約翰的家裏去。
A: It looks like rain. You had better take your raincoat and umbrella with you.	看來快要下雨了。你最好帶着雨衣和雨傘。

2023.mp3

A: What a beautiful day!	天氣多好啊！
B: The weather forecast said it's going to be fine today.	根據天氣預測，今天的天氣將會很好呢。

2024.mp3

A: Is it blowing hard outside?	外面風大嗎？
B: The wind is dying down.	風快停了。
A: And the rain?	還下雨嗎？
B: It looks as if it's going to clear up.	看來天快晴了。

2025.mp3

A: It's very cold today, isn't it?	今天很冷，是不是？
B: Yes, it's freezing and it looks like snow.	是的，真的很冷，看來快要下雪了。
A: We had better stay at home.	我們還是留在家裏吧。

文法及用法説明

❶ 跟別人談及天氣的時候，通常都用附加疑問句（question tags）。當説話的人對陳述句所提到的情況不能完全肯定而需要對方證實時，可用這種疑問句：

It is a fine day, isn't it?	今天天氣真好，可不是嗎？
It looks like rain, doesn't it?	看來是下雨的樣子，可不是嗎？
It isn't cold today, is it?	今天不冷吧，是嗎？
You don't smoke, do you?	你不吸煙的，是嗎？

這類句子的結構是陳述句子加簡短的疑問句而成。陳述句為肯定的，疑問短句則用否定；陳述句為否定的，疑問短句則用肯定。回答這類的問句，要注意Yes和No的用法：

You don't drink, do you?	你不喝酒的，是嗎？
Yes, I do.	不，我喝的。
No, I don't.	是的，我不喝的。
It is hot today, isn't it?	今天很熱，可不是嗎？
Yes, it is.	是的。
No, it isn't.	不是。

❷ It字除了用作代名詞外，還可以用在句首作主語，表示天氣、時間和距離：

It is snowing.	正在下雪。
It is getting dark.	天黑了。
It is four o'clock.	四點鐘了。
It is two years since I last met you.	自從上次見過你到現在有兩年了。
It's two miles to Shatin.	到沙田有兩英里。
It's only a short way from here.	離這裏不遠。

Vocabulary and phrases 生詞

🎧 2026.mp3

temperature	氣溫（溫度）
weatherman	天氣觀測員（天氣報導員）
Thunderstorm is coming.	就要下一場雷雨。
The fog is lifting.	霧開始消散了。
The wind's getting up.	風越來越大了。
It's cloudy.	天氣密雲。
It's fairly cool.	天氣很涼快。
It's bitterly cold.	天氣冷得厲害。
It's quite cold and damp.	天氣陰冷潮濕。

It's breezy and pleasant.	涼風清爽，天氣宜人。
It's muggy and oppressive.	又潮濕又悶熱。
It's a shower.	下着一場陣雨。
It's drizzling.	下着毛毛細雨。
It's raining heavily.	下着大雨。
It's rather changeable.	天氣多變。
It's rather windy.	很大風。
It's sweltering.	熱得使人昏厥。
It's very close and sultry.	天氣很悶熱。
It's warm and sticky.	天氣濕熱黏膩。

3. Introductions 介紹

2031.mp3

A: Miss Wong, allow me to introduce myself.	王小姐，讓我自我介紹吧。
A: My name is john. I'm a friend of your brother's.	我叫約翰，是你兄弟的朋友。
B: Oh, really? I'm very happy to meet you.	啊，真的？很高興認識你。
A: The pleasure is all mine.	我也是。

2032.mp3

A: Excuse me, but may I introduce myself?	對不起，讓我自我介紹一下。
A: My name is Tom. I'm from Hong Kong.	我叫湯姆，我是從香港來的。
B: How do you do❶, Tom? I'm Clarles from Singapore.	湯姆，你好。我叫查里斯，我是從新加坡來的。
A: How do you do, Charles?	查理斯，你好。

2033.mp3

A: Mary, let me introduce Alice to you❷.	瑪麗，讓我介紹愛麗絲給你認識。
A: Alice is a friend of mine.	愛麗絲是我的朋友。
B: Glad to meet you, Alice. Helen has spoken so often of you.	愛麗絲，很高興認識你。
C: Pleased to meet you, too. I hope we shall get to know each other better.	我也很高興認識你。希望我們以後能成為好朋友。

2034.mp3

A: Come on Peter! I'll introduce you to my mother.	彼得，來吧。讓我介紹你給媽媽認識。
A: Mother, this is Peter, my classmate.	媽，這位是我的同學彼得。
M: Hello, PETER! Bob has told me a lot about you.	你好，彼得。鮑勃常常提到你呢。
B: How do you do, Mrs. Li.	李太太，你好。

2035.mp3

A: (Facing C) Mr. Wilson, may I have the pleasure of introducing Mr. Liang to you?	(對C說)威爾遜先生，讓我介紹梁先生給你認識。
A: Mr. Liang is the sales manager of the North-west Company.	梁先生是西北公司的營業經理。
A: (Facing B) Mr. Liang, this is Mr. Wilson of the Trade Development Association.	(對B說)梁先生，這位是貿易發展協會的威爾遜先生。
B: It's a great pleasure to make your acquaintance, Mr. Wilson. I've heard so much about you.	威爾遜先生，很高興認識你。久仰大名了。
C: Thank you, Mr. Liang. I'm very pleased to make your acquaintance, too.	梁先生，謝謝你。我也很高興和你認識。

文法及用法說明

❶ How do you do?（你好。）為初次相識時的寒暄語，形式上是疑問句，但並不要求對方說出健康情況，只要用How do you do?來作回答便可。

❷ 要自我介紹或者介紹別人時，除了課文所提及的句子外還可以用以下的句子：

I'd like to introduce Mr. B.	我想介紹B先生給你。
I'd like you to meet Mr. B.	我想你結識B先生。
May I present Mr. B?	我介紹B先生給你認識好嗎？
Permit me to introduce myself.	容許我介紹自己。

Exercise 練習

2036.mp3

Give responses. 請說出適當的回答。

1. How do you do, Miss Wong?（Mr. Au）
2. How are you, Miss Wong?
3. Merry Christmas and a Happy New Year!
4. Thank you very much.
5. I'm sorry I'm late.

Answer 答案

1. How do you do, Mr. Au?
2. I'm fine, thank you.
3. The same to you.
4. You're welcome./Not at all./Don't mention it.
5. Never mind./That's quite all right.

4. Greetings and regards 招呼、問候

2041.mp3

A: Good morning❶, Mary.	瑪麗，你早。
B: Oh, good morning, Peter.	啊，彼得，你早。
A: How are you❷ today?	你好嗎？
B: I'm just fine, thanks. And you?	很好，謝謝，你呢？
A: I'm fine, too.	我也很好。

2042.mp3

A: I haven't seen you for ages❸. How are you getting on?	好久沒見了，你最近怎麼樣？
B: Quite well, thank you.	很好，謝謝。
A: And how's your family?	府上各位都好嗎？
B: They are all well, thank you.	他們都很好，謝謝你。

2043.mp3

A: Please give my best regards to your father.	請替我問候你的父親。
B: Thank you, I will.	好的，謝謝你。
A: I'm afraid I must say good-bye.	恐怕我現在就要走了。
B: Good-bye. I'll be seeing you.	再見，改天見。

2044.mp3

A: Hello❹, Wong! Where are you going?	你好，老王。上哪兒去呀？
B: Oh, Li. How are you? I'm going to the park	啊，老李，你好嗎？我到公園去呢。

文法及用法説明

❶ Good morning（早晨），Good afternoon（午安），Good evening（晚安）為最普通的招呼用語，無論對任何人都適合，只要注意在恰當的時間應用便可。至於Good night則用於臨別或臨睡之前。

❷ 第一次和人相識互相用How do you do? 來寒暄。以後見面時可以用How are you?, How are you getting on? 對方可以用以下的句子作答：

I'm fine, thank you.	很好，謝謝你。
Quite well, thank you.	
Very well, thanks.	

第二及第三句的主語I'm均被省略掉，這是口語裏常見的情形。至於比較親密的朋友，可以用How's everything?

❸ for ages表示很久、很長的時間。也可以用for years: I haven't seen you for years. 句中的動詞用現在完成式（present perfect tense）。

❹ Hello, Hi 等字只適宜作招呼熟稔朋友之用。

5. Making telephone call 打電話

2051.mp3

A: Hello, Hello!	喂，喂！
B: Hello! Is that 2365-7988?	喂！這裏是2365-7988號嗎？
A: No, it isn't.	不是。
B: Oh, I'm sorry.	啊！對不起。

2052.mp3

A: Hello!	喂！
B: Hello! May I speak to John?	喂！約翰在嗎？
A: One moment, please.	在，請你等一等。
C: Hello! This is John speaking. Is that you, Tom?	喂！我就是約翰。是湯姆嗎？
A: Yes, that's right.	對了，我是湯姆。
A: Mr. Li's office. Who's calling, please?	喂！李先生的辦公室。請問你是誰呀？
B: This is Smith speaking. I wish to talk to Mr. Li.	我是史密斯。我想找李先生。
A: I'm sorry. Mr. Li is on another line.	啊，對不起。李先生在打電話呢。
A: Would you like to leave a message?	你不如留下一個口信好嗎？
B: Please tell him to call me back later.	請你叫李先生一會兒打電話給我好嗎？
A: Yes, I will.	好的。

2053.mp3

A: Hello! Who do you want to speak to?	喂！你找誰呀？
B: Please connect me with Mr. Cheung.	請替我接張先生。
A: I'm sorry. The line's engaged.	對不起，電話佔線了。
A: Would you hold on a moment, please?	請你等一等好嗎？
B: All right.	好的。

文法及用法說明

❶ 找人聽電話，可以有以下的方式：

May I speak to John?	我可以跟約翰談談嗎？
John, please.	請約翰聽電話。
Is John in?	約翰在嗎？
Could I speak to John?	我可以跟約翰談談電話？

❷ 請對方等一等，有以下的方式：

One moment, please.	請等一等。
Hold the line, please.	
Wait a minute, please.	
Just a moment, Please.	

❸ 在電話中通話，問對方「你是誰？」時，要説成Who's speaking (calling)?（誰在説話？）或Who is it?（誰呀？），不能夠用Who are you?。答話的人要説It (This) is...speaking（這是……在説話。），不能夠用I'm...。

❹ 要找的人不在，或者在打另外一個電話，接聽電話的人會説：Can I take a message? 或Would you like to leave a message? 意思是請打電話的人留下一個口信。

Vocabulary 生詞

2054.mp3

cell phone	手提電話
dial	撥（打）電話
extension number	分機號碼
call somebody	打電話給某人。
long distance call	長途電話
make a call	打電話。
mobile (phone)	手提電話
roaming service	漫遊服務
smart phone	智能電話（可上網）
telephone number	電話號碼
The line is busy.	對方電話正在通話。

Exercise 練習

2055.mp3

Listen to the following conversations and answer the questions that follow. 請聽以下對話，然後回答對話後面的問題。

Miss Li is making a phone call. 李小姐正在打電話。

Questions:

1. Who did Miss Li want to speak to?
2. Why couldn't Mr. Wong answer the phone?
3. What does Miss Li have to do later?

Answer 答案

Secretary-S   Miss Li-L

S: Hello, Mr. Wong's office. Can I help you?

L: May I speak to Mr. Wong, please?

S: I'm sorry, Mr. Wong is on another line. Would you like to leave a message?

L: No, I don't think so. I'll call again later.

1. Mr. Wong.
2. Because he was on another line.
3. She has to call again later.

6. Apologies and thanks 道歉、感謝

2061.mp3

A: I'm sorry❶ to have troubled you so much.	麻煩你了，很抱歉。
Thank you for your help.	謝謝你幫忙。
B: Not at all.	哪兒的話。

2062.mp3

A: Excuse me for❷ being so late.	我遲到了，請原諒。
B: Oh, never mind.	啊，不要緊。
A: Have you been waiting long?	你等了很久嗎？
B: No, not too long.	不很久。

2063.mp3

A: It's very kind of you to come here.	你來了，真好。
A: Thank you very much.	謝謝你呀。
B: The pleasure is all mine.	我十分樂意到這兒來呢。

2064.mp3

A: Sorry to disturb you, but could you spare me a few minutes?	打擾你了，對不起。可以佔你幾分鐘嗎？
B: Certainly.	不要緊。

2065.mp3

A: I apologize❸ for what I did yesterday. It was my fault.	昨天的事，真抱歉。那是我的錯。
B: Let's forget it❹.	忘記吧。

文法及用法說明

❶ I'm sorry 的意思是「對不起」、「抱歉」，含義大致上和 excuse me、pardon me 相同。I'm sorry 通常用於婉拒他人的餽贈或要求，或者用來表示不同意別人的意見，和道出自己內心的不安等等。Excuse me 亦作「對不起」解，在給別人一點小麻煩時用，例如請人讓路，表示要走開，向別人問路或時間等。英國人習慣用 excuse，而 pardon 則是美國人的常用語。

❷ 如果要說明請求原諒的原因，可以在 excuse me 或 sorry 之後加上 for，再加名詞或動名詞(gerund)：

Excuse me for my interruption. Excuse me for interrupting you. Sorry for interrupting you. Sorry to interrupt you.	請原諒我打擾你。

interruption 為名詞，interrupting 為動句詞；另外 sorry 之後可以用帶 to 的動詞不定式(infinitive)。Thank you 之後也可以加上 for，以表示感謝別人的原因：

Thank you for your invitation. Thank you for inviting me.	謝謝你的邀請。

❸ 犯了嚴重的過失，請求人家饒恕時，要用 apologize:

I apologize for making such a mistake.	我犯了這樣的錯誤，實在抱歉。

也可以說：

Please forgive me.	請饒恕我。

❹ 別人表示歉意時，最普通的答語為 That's all right 或者 It's all right。Forget it 則用於較為親密的朋友。

7. Congratulations 祝賀

2071.mp3

A: I understand you and Mary are engaged.	我知道你已經跟瑪麗訂了婚了。
B: Yes, we're going to be married in June.	是的，我們準備六月結婚。
A: Congratulations❶! I hope you'll be very happy.	恭喜你！祝你快樂。
B: Thanks.	謝謝你。

2072.mp3

A: Say, I hear you passed the examination.	聽說你考試及格了。
B: Yes, I guess I'm just lucky.	啊，我猜我只是有些運氣。
A: Well, congratulations!	那麼恭喜你啊！
B: Thank you so much.	謝謝你。

2073.mp3

A: Say, I hear you got a job at the National Bank.	聽説你在國家銀行找到一份工作。
B: Yes, I start work next week.	是的。下個星期開始上班。
A: That's great! Congratulations!	多好！恭喜你啊！
B: Thanks. How about you? Didn't you apply for a job in a trading company?	謝謝。那麼你呢？你不是向一家貿易公司申請了一份工作嗎？
A: Yes, I've got an interview next week.	是的。下個星期參加面試。

B: Well, I wish❷ you the best of luck.	那麼，祝你幸運。
A: Thanks.	謝謝。

2074.mp3

A: I hear it's your birthday today, Mr. Li.	李先生，聽說今天是你的生日。
B: That's right.	對。
A: Congratulations and many happy returns of the day.	恭祝你年年有今日，歲歲有今朝。
B: Thanks very much.	謝謝你。

文法及用法說明

❶ 向某人祝賀，最簡單的用語為 Congratulations! 如果要表示祝賀的理由，可以用以下的方式：

I congratulate you on your marriage.	我恭祝你們婚姻美滿。
Congratulations on your passing the examination!	恭喜你考試及格！
Congratulations on your promotion!	恭喜你升級！
Congratulations on your getting a new job!	恭喜你得到一份新工作！

遇到節日或特別的日子，可以說：

Merry Christmas!	聖誕快樂！
Happy New Year!	新年快樂！

回答的時候要說：

Thank you, (the) same to you.	謝謝你，你也一樣吧。

❷ wish是祝福別人的用語：

I wish you a pleasant journey.	祝你旅途愉快。
Best wishes!	祝福你！
I wish you every success in your new job!	祝你工作愉快！

8. Condolences 慰問

2081.mp3

A: I've just heard about the death in your family. I'm very sorry.	聽到你一位家人逝世的消息，我十分難過。
B: Yes, my grandfather passed away❶.	是的，我的祖父逝世了。
A: Please accept my condolences❷.	請接受我的哀悼。
B: Thank you very much for your sympathy.	謝謝你的關心。

2082.mp3

A: What's the matter with you? You look a little downcast.	你怎麼啦？好像不太開心。
B: Oh, I've just got the results of the final examination.	我剛剛接到考試的成績。
B: I've failed.	不及格了。
A: That's too bad. I'm sorry to hear that.	真倒霉，聽到了我真替你難過。
B: I guess it's my own fault. I didn't study enough.	我想這是我的過失。我準備不夠充份。
Well, I can always try again.	那麼，我總可以繼續努力呀。

2083.mp3

A: I heard about your father. I'm very sorry.	聽到你父親逝世的消息，我十分難過。
B: Thanks, John.	謝謝你，約翰。
A: If there's anything I can do, please tell me.	要是有什麼我可以幫忙的，請你儘管告訴我好了。
B: Thanks. I think we can take care of everything.	謝謝。我想我們可以照顧一切的。
A: And please give my condolences to your mother.	請替我慰問一下你的母親。
B: Thank you, John.	謝謝你，約翰。

文法及用法說明

❶ pass away的意思為逝世，語氣較die（死亡）為婉轉。

❷ 聽到不幸的消息，向別人慰問，可以用以下的語句：

Please accept my condolences.	請接受我的哀悼。
Please accept my deepest sympathy.	我十分同情你。
I was very sorry to hear of your sister's death.	聽到你姊姊逝世的消息，我很難過。

9. Paying visits 探訪

2091.mp3

A: Good morning. Is Mr. Wu in❶?	你早，胡先生在家嗎？
B: Yes sir. What name shall I say?	在。你貴姓呀？
A: My name is Liu. I'd like to see Mr. Wu.	我姓劉，我想見見胡先生。
B: One moment, please. I'll go and see.	請你等一等，我去看看。
A: Thank you.	謝謝你。

2092.mp3

A: Is this Miss Wong's residence?	這兒是王小姐的家嗎？
B: Yes, madam. But I'm afraid that that Miss Wong is out❷.	是的，太太。可是王小姐出去了。
B: May I have your name?	你貴姓呀？
A: I'm White. Please tell Miss Wong that I called.	我姓韋。請告訴王小姐我找過她。
B: All right, I will.	好的，我告訴她。

2093.mp3

A: Good afternoon.	你好。
B: Good afternoon, John. It's nice to see you.	約翰，你好。很高興見到你，
B: Please come in.	請進來坐。
A: I was just passing by, so I dropped in❸.	我剛好經過這裏，順便來坐坐。

B: Oh, that's good of you. Let me take your coat.	你有心了。把你的外套給我吧。

🎧 2094.mp3

A: Is your father at home?	你父親在家嗎？
B: No, I'm sorry. But he'll be back at six.	對不起，他不在家。不過他六點鐘就回來。
A: I will call❹ later.	那麼我一會兒再來吧。
B: Who shall I say wishes to see him?	你貴姓呀？
A: I'm Fung. Here is my card.	我姓馮。這是我的名片。

PART 02

文法及用法說明

❶ Is...in? 用來詢問某人是否在家，相同意思的句子還有 Is...at home? 如果初次到訪，對地址不大肯定的話，可以用 Is this Miss Li's residence?（這是李小姐的家嗎？）或Does Miss Li live here?（李小姐住在這兒嗎？）。

❷ ...is out 的意思為不在家，出去了；亦可以說 ...is not in 或 ...is not at home。

❸ drop in 的意思為順便走訪。例如：

Would you drop in (on us) tomorrow evening for a chat?	你明晚有便來（和我們一起）談談好嗎？

❹ call 在此為拜訪的意思：

I called on him.	我拜訪了他。

I called at his house.	我曾到他的家拜訪了他。
I called to see him.	我曾拜訪他。
He was out when I called.	當我往訪時，適值他出去了。

Exercise 練習

2095.mp3

Answer the following questions. 請回答下列問題。

1. Where are you going?（to the park）
2. Where did he go yesterday?（to the library）
3. Where does she live?（in Hong Kong）
4. Where's your book?（on the desk）
5. Where did you put your book?（on the bookshelf）

Answer 答案

1. I am going to the park.
2. He went to the library yesterday.
3. She lives in Hong Kong.
4. It's on the desk.
5. I put it on the bookshelf.

10. Appointments 約會

2101.mp3

A: May I come and see you this evening?	我今天晚上來探望你好不好？
B: Oh, I'm sorry, but I have another appointment.	哎呀，對不起，我已經有一個約會呢。
B: Could you make it tomorrow morning?	明天早上行嗎？
A: Yes, that would be fine.	行，就這樣吧。

PART 02

2102.mp3

A: Dr. Chan's office.	陳醫生醫務所。
B: This is Mr. Wu. I'd like to make an appointment for❶ a check-up.	我姓胡，我想跟醫生約一個時間檢查身體。
A: How about Tuesday, the 8th, at ten o'clock?	八號，星期二，十點鐘，行嗎？
B: I'm sorry, but I have an engagement on Tuesday morning❷.	啊，對不起，我星期二早上有一個約會呢。
A: How would Thursday be?	星期四怎麼樣？
B: Thursday would be fine.	星期四很好。
A: Thursday at ten, then.	那麼就給你定了星期四，十點鐘了。
B: Thank you very much. Good-bye.	謝謝你，再見。

2103.mp3

A: I thought we might have lunch and go to the cinema this afternoon.	今天下午我們一起吃午飯，然後看電影，你認為怎麼樣？
B: I'd love to! Where shall we meet?	好極了！我們在什麼地方見面？
A: Shall we have lunch at Jimmy's Restaurant?	我們去占美餐廳吃午飯好不好？
A: They serve good food there.	那兒的菜不錯呢。
B: Good idea! Let's meet at Jimmy's at one o'clock.	好主意！我們一點鐘在占美餐廳見面吧。
A: Fine. See you later.	好，等會兒見。
B: All right.	好的。

2104.mp3

A: Good morning, sir. May I help you?	先生，你早。我可以幫你的忙嗎？
B: Yes, my name is William Li, and I have an appointment with Mr. Hawkins at 11:30.	可以。我叫李威廉。我跟霍金斯先生在十一點半有一個約會。
A: Oh, yes, Mr. Li. Would you please take a seat.	啊，李先生，是啊，請坐一會兒。
A: I will tell Mr. Hawkins that you are here.	我通知霍金斯先生說你來了。
B: Thank you.	謝謝你。

A: Please go right in, Mr. Li. Mr. Hawkins is expecting you.	李先生請進去。霍金斯先生等着見你了。
B: Thank you very much.	謝謝。

PART 02

文法及用法説明

❶ make an appointment for... 意思為：為了某事而定一個約會，例如：

He has made an appointment for a medical examination.	他約好了時間檢查身體。

如果要表示跟某人約好了時間，可以説：

He has made an appointment with the dentist at 2:00p.m.	他約好了下午兩點鐘去看牙醫。
He has made an appointment to see the dentist at 2:00p.m.	

❷ 與人約會，常常會談及到日期和時間，要特別注意前置詞（prepositions）的運用：

in 1999	在一九九九年
in autumn	在秋天
in September	在九月份
on the first of May	五月一日
on Monday	星期一

at two o'clock	兩點鐘
on New Year's Eve	除夕
in the morning	早上
in the afternoon	下午
in the evening	晚上
at noon	中午
at night	夜間
at midnight	午夜

Exercise 練習

2105.mp3

Listen to the following conversations and answer the questions that follow. 請聽以下對話，然後回答對話後面的問題。

A girl is making an appointment with Mr. Smith. 一個女孩正在約定時間跟史密斯先生見面。

Questions:

1. What was the girl's name?
2. Who did she want to see?
3. Was Mr. Smith very busy?
4. When is Mr. Smith free?

Answer 答案

Girl-G　　Secretary-S

G: I'd like to see Mr. Smith, please.
S: Do you have an appointment?
G: No, I don't. I've just arrived today.
S: Mr. Smith is quite busy today.
G: Do you think I could see him tomorrow?
S: Let me check his appointments. Let's see.
He's free at 2:30 tomorrow afternoon. Would that be all right?
G: Yes, I can make it at 2:30.
S: What is your name, please?
G: Mary Wong.

1. Mary Wong.
2. Mr. Smith.
3. Yes, he was.
4. 2:30 p.m. the next day.

11. Invitations 邀請

2111.mp3

A: Are you free next Sunday?	你下星期日有空嗎？
B: Yes, I am.	有的。
A: We're having a dinner party. Would you like to join us?	我們準備開一個晚會，你參加嗎？
B: Oh, I'd love to❶.	我十分喜歡參加。
A: Could you come at six o'clock?	六點鐘來行嗎？
B: Certainly.	行。

2112.mp3

A: Could you come to dinner tomorrow evening?	你明天晚上可以來吃晚飯嗎？
B: Thank you for your kind invitation, but I'm afraid I can't.	謝謝你的好意，不過我恐怕不能來。
B: I have a previous engagement.	我已經有一個約會了。
A: Oh, what a pity!	啊，太可惜了！

2113.mp3

A: Good evening, Mr. Chan.	陳先生，你好。
B: Good evening, Mrs. Li. Please come in.	李太太，你好。請進來吧。
A: Thank you.	謝謝你。
B: It's good of you❷ to come, Mrs. Li.	李太太，謝謝你光臨。
A: It was very kind of you to invite me.	我該謝謝你的好意呢。

PART 02

文法及用法説明

❶ 人家以口頭或電話邀請赴宴，如果答應的話，可以説： Oh, I'd love to 或者 Certainly, I will be delighted to. 要是不能赴宴，應首先表示感謝，並説明理由。

❷ 要注意 good of you 及 good for you 的分別。good of you 意為「你真好」，而 good for you 意為「對你有益」。

12. Entertaining guests 招待

2121.mp3

A: Won't you have some more potatoes?	你還要點馬鈴薯嗎？
B: No, thank you. They're delicious, but I've had enough❶ already.	不要了，謝謝你。這些馬鈴薯很可口。
A: How about some salad?	要點沙拉嗎？
B: No, this will be fine.	不要了，這些已經夠了。
A: Are you on a diet❷ or something?	你在節食嗎？
B: No, but I am trying to cut down on my calories.	不是，我不過在減少熱量吧了。

2122.mp3

A: Well, shall we have our coffee in the other room?	我們到那邊喝咖啡好不好？
B: Yes, let's. I think it'll be more comfortable in there.	好，我們去吧。那兒比較舒適呢。
A: Thank you very much for the dinner. It was delicious.	謝謝你請我來吃晚飯，那些菜式真美味。
B: Glad you enjoyed it.	你喜歡，我很高興。

2123.mp3

A: Hello there. Having a good time?	喂！玩得開心嗎？
B: Oh, yes. It's a lovely party.	很開心。這個聚會可熱鬧啊！
A: Say, can't I get you a Martini or something?	我給你拿點馬天尼酒還是什麼來好嗎？
B: No, thank you. I don't drink.	不用了，謝謝你，我不喝酒的。
A: Then how about❸ some grape juice?	那麼，要點葡萄汁怎麼樣？
B: All right. That would be very nice.	好，這個倒很好。

PART 02

文法及用法説明

❶ enough的意思為足夠、充分。在本課，have enough的意思為「吃飽了」，例如：Thank you, I've had more than enough.（謝謝你，我已經吃得很飽了。）表示吃飽，又可以説I'm full.

❷ on a diet原指一個人因為某種理由（例如醫療的理由）而被限制飲食，例如：The doctor put her on a diet.（醫生限制她的飲食。）現在多應用作「節食」之意。

❸ How about...?意為「……怎麼樣？」也可以寫成What about...?

Vocabulary 生詞

2124.mp3

beverages	飲料
beer	啤酒
brandy	白蘭地
champagne	香檳酒
cider	蘋果酒
cocktail	雞尾酒
draught beer	生啤酒
gin	松子酒（氈酒）
ginger wine	薑酒
martini	馬天尼酒
liquor/spirit	烈酒
red/white wine	紅/白葡萄酒
sherry	雪莉酒
vodka	伏特加
whisky	威士忌

13. Tea time 喝茶

2131.mp3

A: Tea is ready, George. Come this way, please.	喬治，茶預備好了，請到這邊來吧。
B: Thanks for inviting me.	謝謝你的邀請。
A: How would you like your tea? Will you have milk and sugar?	要在茶裏放點甚麼嗎？放點牛奶和糖好嗎？
B: Just sugar, please.	請放點糖吧。

2132.mp3

A: How many lumps❶?	幾塊？
B: Two, please. The tea is very good.	兩塊吧。這茶很好喝。
A: I'm glad you like it. Help yourself to me cakes.	你喜歡，我很高興。隨便吃點糕點吧。
B: Thank you.	謝謝。
A: Won't you have some more cakes?	還要糕點嗎？
B: No more, thank you. I've had enough.	不要了，謝謝你。我已經飽啦。

2133.mp3

A: This is a very nice coffee shop. Do you come here often?	這家咖啡館很好，你常常來嗎？
B: I usually drop in here whenever I happen❷ to be in this part of town.	每當我到這一區來的時候，我總是順道進來坐坐。
Well, what shall I order for you?	噢，你想吃點甚麼呢？

A: Just coffee, please.	一杯咖啡就夠了。
B: How about some cakes? The French pastry they serve here is exceptionally good.	吃些糕點如何？這裏的法國式糕餅做得特別好。
A: No, thanks. I have to watch my waistline.	不要了，謝謝你。我得注意我的體重。
B: Really? You don't look overweight to me at all.	真的？你看來一點也不超重呢。
A: Thanks.	謝謝你。

🎧 2134.mp3

A: Here's the milk and sugar.	這是牛奶和糖。
B: No, thanks. I like my coffee black❸.	不用了，謝謝你。我喜歡喝黑咖啡。
A: Oh, I see. But for me, I always put in two lumps of sugar and lots of milk.	原來是這樣。我倒喜歡放兩塊方糖，還加很多的牛奶呢。

文法及用法説明

❶ lumps是塊的意思。a lump of（一塊），例如： a lump of sugar（一塊方糖）。英文裏的不可數名詞（uncountable nouns）有單位的固定叫法，例如： a piece of paper（一張紙），a piece of bread（一片麵包），a glass of water（一杯水）……。

❷ happen 為碰巧的意思，例如： I happened to be out when he called.（他到訪時，碰巧我出去了。），It so happened that I had no money with me.（剛巧我身上沒有錢。）

❸ black coffee 為不加牛奶的咖啡。

Vocabulary 生詞

2135.mp3

café	咖啡館
cocoa	可可
coffee	咖啡
black coffee	黑咖啡
coffee with milk	牛奶咖啡
cappuccino	肉桂牛奶咖啡
espresso	特濃咖啡
iced coffee	冰咖啡
mocha	巧克力咖啡
fruit juice	果汁
fruit punch	雜果賓治
lemonade	檸檬水
ice-cream sundae	雪糕新地
milkshake	奶昔
tea	茶
Earl Grey tea	百爵茶
green tea	綠茶
jasmine tea	茉莉花茶
oolong tea	烏龍茶

14. At the restaurant 餐館晚餐

At the Restaurant 餐館

2141.mp3

A: What's the name of this restaurant?	這家餐館叫甚麼名字？
B: It's King's Restaurant. What do you think of it?	皇室餐廳。你覺得怎麼樣？
A: The food is excellent❶.	這兒的菜式很好。
B: I think so❷, too. And this is a good steak.	我同意。這牛排味道很美。
Will you pass the mustard, please?	請把芥醬遞給我。
A: Yes, here it is. Shall we order another bottle of beer?	喏，給你。再來一瓶啤酒好嗎？
B: By all means.	很好。
A: Waiter, another bottle of beer, please.	夥計，給我們再來一瓶啤酒。

2142.mp3

A: What are you going to have, Jack?	傑克，你吃些甚麼呢？
B: Well, I don't know. Let's see the menu.	我不知道。我們先看看菜單吧。
A: I think I'd like a club sandwich.	我要一客公司三文治。
B: Do they have any tuna fish?	不知道這兒有吞拿魚沒有呢？
A: I'm afraid not. But there's salmon salad.	恐怕沒有。不過他們有三文魚沙律。

B: That'll be all right. Do you want coffee?	這個倒很好。你喝咖啡嗎？
A: I'll have Coca Cola if they've got it.	要是有可樂的話，就來一杯可樂吧。
B: (To waiter) One Club sandwich, one salmon salad sandwich, one coffee and one Coca Cola, please.	(對侍應說) 給我們來一客公司三文治、一客三文魚沙律三文治、一杯咖啡跟一杯可樂。

PART 02

文法及用法説明

❶ 要讚美食物美味可口時，最常用的語句是It's delicious. 或者It's excellent.

❷ 在口語，so常常用作say, think等動詞的賓語 (object)：

I think so.	我同意。
I don't think so.	我不同意。
I hope so.	希望如此。
I suppose so.	我以為如此。
You don't say so?	你不同意嗎？
I believe so.	我相信是這樣。

so在口語，常用做「亦」、「也」等的意思：

You were wrong and so was I.	你固然有錯，我亦有誤。
She sings beautifully and so does he.	她唱歌唱得很好，他也是。
He went there yesterday and so did I.	他昨天到那裏去，我也去了。

Dinner 晚餐

2143.mp3

A: I'm glad you were able to come, Mr. Li.	李先生，你真賞臉。
I know how busy you are.	我知道你十分忙呢。
B: I'm never too busy to have dinner with you, Mrs. Jones.	瓊斯先生請客，我一定抽空來的。
A: It's very kind of you to say so.	你太客氣了。
How about having a cocktail first, to whet our appetite?	先喝點雞尾酒刺激一下胃口怎麼樣？
B: Splendid! I'll have a Martini.	好極了！我要一杯馬丁尼酒。
A: I'll have the same.	跟你一樣吧。
(After a while 過了一會兒)	
A: Are you ready to order now?	現在可以點菜了嗎？
B: Yes, I think so.	可以啦。
A: Oh, waiter. Menu, please.	夥計，拿菜單給我們看看。
Waiter: Very good, sir.	好的，先生。
A: Which soup do you prefer, Mr. Li?	李先生，你喜歡喝甚麼湯？
B: I think I'll have the French onion soup.	我要一客法國洋葱湯。
A: That sounds❶ good to me, too.	這湯也很適合我。

Waiter, two orders of French onion soup.	夥計，給我們兩客法國洋葱湯吧。
W: Yes, sir.	好的，先生。
A: Next, I think I'll have the lobster. How about you, Mr. Li?	跟着來一客龍蝦。李先生，你怎麼樣呢？
B: I'd rather❷ have the fried garoupa with white sauce.	我還是要一客白汁炸石斑魚。
It's my favourite dish.	這是我最愛吃的菜。
A: Before the fish, shall we also have some hors d'oeuvres?	我們先來一客冷盤再吃魚，好不好？
B: That would be very nice.	十分好。
A: For the main course, I think I'll have a sirloin steak.	我想要一客西冷牛排作主菜。
B: How would you like it (done)? Would you like it rare, medium, or well-done?	你喜歡牛排怎麼做？你喜歡做得生一點，半熟，或是全熟？
A: Medium, please.	我要半熟吧。
B: That sounds awfully good to me. I'll have the same.	這個菜十分適合我。跟你一樣吧。
(Some moments later 稍後)	
A: What would you like for dessert, Mr. Li?	李先生，你要些甚麼甜品嗎？
B: I'm afraid I'll have to skip the dessert, Mrs. Jones.	恐怕吃不下了，瓊斯太太。

But I would like to have some coffee.	不過我想喝點咖啡。
A: All right. And how about some brandy to top off❸ the meal?	好的。我們最後來些白蘭地酒如何？
B: That sounds good.	這主意不錯。

文法及用法説明

❶ sounds在這裏作動詞用，有「聽起來……」及「似乎」的意思：

How sweet the music sounds!	這音樂聽起來多悦耳！
That explanation sounds all right.	這個解釋似乎很合理。

❷ would rather用來表示對某事物的優先選擇：

I'd rather have this one than that one.	我寧可要這個不要那個。
I'd rather you stayed here.	我寧願你留在這裏。

如果做動作的人不是説話者本身，動詞就要用過去式，例如上面第二句中的stayed.

表示優先選擇，又可以用prefer to:

He prefers swimming to hiking.	他比較喜歡游泳勝過遠足。
I prefer doing this to doing that.	我寧可做這事不做那事。

❸ to top off的意思為「完成」、「結束」。

Vocabulary 生詞

2144.mp3

chef suggestion / recommendation	廚師推介
today special	即日精選
a la carte	從餐牌點菜
western cuisine	西餐
appetizer	前菜（開胃菜）
salad	沙律（沙拉）
salad dressing	沙律醬

2145.mp3

main course	主菜
steak	牛排
rib-eye steak	肉眼排
sirloin steak	西冷排
t-bone steak	T骨排
rare	生一點（二成熟）
medium rare	三至四成熟
medium	半熟（五成熟）
well-done	全熟

2146.mp3

soup	湯
borsch	羅宋湯
clam chowder	周打蜆湯
chicken soup	雞湯
consommé	清燉肉湯
cream of mushroom	忌廉磨菇湯
minestrone	意大利菜湯
onion soup	洋葱湯
tomato soup	番茄湯

2147.mp3

grilled chicken	燒雞
lamp chop	羊排
pork chop	豬排
roast beef	燒牛肉
sandwich	三文治
ketchup	茄汁
worcestershire sauce	喼汁

2148.mp3

Chinese cuisine	中餐
abalone slices with oyster sauce	蠔油鮑片
barbecued pork	叉燒
Beijing roast duck	北京填鴨
crispy fried chicken	炸子雞
eggplant in Sichuan style	魚香茄子
sweet and sour pork	甜酸肉排（咕嚕肉）
roast suckling pig	燒乳豬
prawns with ketchup	茄汁蝦
scrambled egg with shrimps	蝦仁炒蛋
shark's fin soup	魚翅湯
tender boiled chicken with soy sauce	豉油雞

15. Health 健康

2151.mp3

A: Hello, Mary! How are you!	喂！瑪麗，你好嗎？
B: Fine, thank you. And you?	很好，謝謝你。你呢？
A: I haven't been feeling too well recently.	近來我的身體不大好。
I've had❶ a severe stomachache.	我的胃痛得很厲害呢。
B: I'm sorry to hear that. Are you all right now?	聽到了也真替你擔心。現在沒事吧？
A: Yes, I feel better❷ now. Thank you.	沒有甚麼啦，謝謝你。

2152.mp3

A: You are looking rather pale. Anything wrong?	你的臉色很蒼白，有甚麼事嗎？
B: I feel rather dizzy.	我覺得有點頭暈。
A: You must lie down for a while.	躺下來歇一會兒吧。
B: All right. Thank you.	好的，謝謝你。
A: Shall I call❸ a doctor?	替你找醫生好嗎？
B: No, I think I'll be all right in a minute.	不用了。我休息一會兒就沒事了。

2153.mp3

A: How do you feel today?	今天覺得怎麼樣？
B: Oh, I feel much better, thank you.	我覺得精神好了很多。謝謝你。

A: That's good. When can you come home?	那就好了。甚麼時候可以出院呢？
B: Pretty❹ soon, I think.	很快就可以出院了。
It's very kind of you to come and see me.	你來探望我，真有心。
A: Not at all.	哪兒的話。

PART 02

文法及用法說明

❶ have在本課裏的意思與suffer from（患病）相同。例如：

He had a headache yesterday.	昨天他覺得頭痛。
Do you often have colds?	你時常感冒嗎？

❷ better為well的比較級，well為副詞（adverb）。通常副詞比較級的形式為more+副詞原形：

Please run more slowly.	請跑慢一點。
Drive more carefully this time.	這一次要小心點駕駛。

❸ call: 為召喚的意思，亦可以用send for代替之：

Please send for a doctor.	請找醫生來。

❹ pretty在這裏作副詞用，通常用於口語，意思為「相當多」、「頗多」：

It's pretty warm today.	今天天氣甚暖。
The dish is pretty good.	這道菜十分美味。

Vocabulary and phrases 生詞

2154.mp3

do not feel good	感到不舒服
feel dizzy	頭暈眼花
feel pain	感到疼痛
have a bad cough	咳得很厲害
have a stuffed-up nose	感到鼻塞
have got a headache	感到頭痛
have got a toothache	感到牙痛
have got a stomach-ache	感到胃痛
have got a flu	患上流行性感冒
have insomnia	失眠
have ringing in the ear	耳鳴
vomit	嘔吐

Exercise 練習

2155.mp3

Answer the following questions. 請回答下列問題。

1. How old are you? (twenty)
2. How much is it? (ten dollars)
3. How high is that building? (thirty stories)
4. How tall are you? (five feet four inches)
5. How long is this road? (five miles)

Answer 答案

1. I'm twenty years old.
2. It's ten dollars.
3. It's thirty stories high.
4. I'm five feet four inches tall.
5. It's five miles long.

16. Seeing the doctor 看病

2161.mp3

A: Excuse me. I'd like to see a doctor.	對不起，我想看病。
Nurse: Do you have an appointment, sir?	你有沒有約定時間呢，先生？
A: No. This is my first visit.	沒有。我是第一次來的。
N: I see. Will you fill out this card, please?	哦，原來是這樣。請你填好這張卡片。
A: Yes...Here it is.	好的……填好了。
N: Please go to the waiting room, and wait there until your name is called.	請你到候診室去等一會兒，我們會叫你的名字的。
A: All right. Thank you.	好的，謝謝你。
N: Mr. White, Mr. John White!	懷特先生，約翰・懷特先生。
A: I'm John White.	我就是了。
N: Please follow me. The doctor will see you now.	請跟我來。醫生現在要見你啦。
A: Thank you.	謝謝你。
Doctor: Sit down here. Now what seems to be the trouble?	請坐。有甚麼問題呢？
A: I don't feel well. I'm tired all the time and can't sleep well.	我覺得很不舒服。整天都很累，夜裏又睡得不好。
D: Anything else?	還有呢？
A: No. Just feeling tired. Even in the morning when I first wake up.	我只覺得累就是了。一清早起來就有這種感覺。
D: Well, your body temperature is quite normal.	你的體溫很正常。

Let me hear your breathing	讓我聽聽你的呼吸。
A: Am I all right?	沒有問題吧？
D: Yes. Well, it may just be due to❶ the change in weather.	沒有。這可能是天氣變化所引起的。
Be sure to eat regularly and get lots of rest. I'll give you a prescription.	你要按時進食，還要多多休息。我給你開張藥方。
A: Thank you for seeing me, doctor.	謝謝你，醫生。

PART 02

At the Pharmacy 在配藥部

2162.mp3

A: Excuse me. Here's my prescription.	對不起，這是我的藥方。
N: Please sit over there and we'll call you.	請坐一會兒，我們會叫你的名字。
A: Thank you.	謝謝你。
N: Mr. John White!	約翰・懷特先生。
A: That's me. I'm John White.	我就是了，我就是約翰・懷特。
N: Here's your medicine. You take two of these tablets every four hours❷.	這是你的藥。每四小時吃兩片。
A: I understand. Where do I pay for these?	我知道了。哪裏付錢呢？
N: At the cashier. That window over there.	到收款處去吧，就在那邊的窗口。
A: Thank you.	謝謝你。

文法及用法說明

❶ due to 的意思為「由於」、「起因於」，不可以放在句首，一定要與動詞be連用：

The accident was due to his carelessness.	這意外起因於他的疏忽。

Owing to也有同樣的意思，但必須放在句首：

Owing to his carelessness, we had an accident.	由於他疏忽，我們發生了車禍。

以上的句子也可以用because代替：

We had an accident because he was careless.	因為他疏忽，我們發生了車禍。

❷ 如果要表示每逢一段時間便要發生的事，可以用every一字，例如：

every day	每天
every year	每年
every morning	每早
every two days	每兩天
every ten years	每十年
every other day	每隔一天
every two weeks	每兩週

Vocabulary and phrases 生詞

2163.mp3

asthma	哮喘
blood pressure	血壓
chronic disease	慢性病
common illness	常見疾病
constipation	便秘
contagious disease	傳染病
cough	咳嗽
cramp	痙攣
diabetes	糖尿病
gastric hyperacidity	胃酸過多
gastritis	胃炎
have loose bowels	肚瀉
hypertension	高血壓
stroke	中風
sore throat	喉嚨痛
(have) indigestion	消化不良
inflammation	發炎
pregnant	懷孕

Exercise 練習

2164.mp3

Listen to the following conversations and answer the questions that follow. 請聽以下對話，然後回答對話後面的問題。

Two schoolmates are talking to each other. 兩位同學正在談話。

Questions:

1. What was wrong with the girl?
2. Did she see a doctor?
3. What did the doctor advise her to do?
4. Does she feel better today?

Answer 答案

A: I caught a bad cold yesterday.

B: I'm sorry to hear that. Are you feeling better now?

A: Yes, much better, thank you.
I went to see the doctor and he gave me a prescription.

B: What did he say?

A: He told me to take things easy and drink more water.

1. She had a bad cold.
2. Yes, she did.
3. He advised her to take things easy and drink more water.
4. Yes, she does.

17. At the department store 百貨公司

2171.mp3

A: May I help you, sir?	先生，要買東西嗎？
B: Yes, I want a pair of brown leather shoes.	是的，我想買一雙棕色的皮鞋。
A: What size❶, sir?	甚麼尺碼的，先生？
B: Size seven, I think.	我想是七號吧。
A: Here's a pair about your size. How do you like these?	這裏有一雙很適合你，你喜歡不喜歡？
They are the latest❷ style.	這是最新的款式。
B: I don't think I like them. Show me another, please!	我不太喜歡，拿另外一雙給我看看吧。

2172.mp3

A: Good afternoon, madam. What can I do for you?	太太，午安。要買東西嗎？
B: Could you please show me that doll over there?	請你拿那邊的洋娃娃給我看看好嗎？
A: Certainly, madam. Here you are.	好的，太太。這就是了。
B: How much is it❸?	賣多少錢？
A: Two hundred dollars, madam.	二百元，太太。
B: All right, I'll take it.	好的，我就買這個吧。
A: Anything else, madam?	還要別的東西嗎，太太？
B: No, thank you. That's all.	沒有甚麼啦，我要的就這麼多。

A: Can I help you, sir?	先生，要買東西嗎？
B: Yes, I'm looking for a birthday present for my sister in Canada.	是的，我想買一份生日禮物送給住在加拿大的妹妹。
How much is that brooch?	那個別針賣多少錢？
A: Four Hundred dollars, sir.	四百塊，先生。
B: I'll take it. Could you gift-wrap it and send it for me?	好，我買。請你替我包好，寄去加拿大。
I want it to go by courier.	請寄速遞吧。
A: I'm sorry, sir, but you'll have to go to the packing and wrapping department.	對不起，先生，請你到禮品包裝部去吧！
There's a small charge for it.	我們只收取少許的費用。

2173.mp3

B: That's all right. Where is it?	不要緊。包裝部在哪兒呢？
A: It's over there near the elevator.	在那邊，電梯附近。
B: Thank you.	謝謝你。

文法及用法説明

❶ 顧客在選購物品時，售貨員通常都會提出以下的問題：

What size do you take?	你要甚麼尺碼的？
What colour do you prefer?	你要甚麼顏色的？
What quality do you like?	你喜歡甚麼質地的？
Do you have any particular brand in mind?	你心目中想要甚麼牌子？

❷ latest為「最新」、「最近」的意思，為形容詞late（近來）的最高級形式。例： the latest news（最新的消息），the latest fashions（最近時尚的），his latest works（他最新的作品）。

❸ 要詢問價格，可以用以下的問句：

What's the price?	它賣甚麼價錢？
How much does it cost?	它價值多少？
How much do you charge for it?	這個要多少錢？

注意cost作為名詞時，不可以用來詢問價錢：例如What's the cost of this watch? 意思指「這隻錶的成本是多少？」談到價錢便宜或昂貴時，可以説：

The price of this watch is too high (low).	這隻錶的價錢太貴（便宜）了。
This watch is too expensive (cheap).	這隻錶太貴（便宜）了。

Vocabulary and phrases 生詞

2174.mp3

art and crafts	工藝美術
books	書籍
food and wine	食物、酒類
home furnishing	家居裝飾用品
home electronics	家居電子用品
kitchen appliances	廚房用具
men's clothing	男裝
music and movies	音樂電影
toys and stationery	玩具與文具
watches and jewellery	手錶、珠寶首飾
women's clothing	女裝
shoes	皮鞋
toiletries	浴室用品
sports wear	運動服裝

Exercise 練習

2175.mp3

Listen to the following conversations and answer the questions that follow. 請聽以下對話，然後回答對話後面的問題。

A customer wants to buy a shirt in a department store. 一位顧客在百貨公司裏選襯衣。

Questions:

1. What did the customer want to buy?
2. What colour did she want?
3. How much is the shirt?
4. Did she buy the shirt?

Answer 答案

Store Clerk-SC   Customer-C

SC: Good morning. May I help you?
C: Yes. Could you please show me that shirt over there?
SC: Certainly, madam. It's made of cotton.
C: Do you have the same thing in brown?
SC: Yes. Here you are, madam.
C: How much is it?
SC: Fifty dollars, madam.
C: O.K. I'll have this one.

1. a shirt
2. Brown
3. Fifty dollars
4. Yes, she did.

18. At the supermarket 超級市場

2181.mp3

A: What are you going to buy first?	你先要買些甚麼東西呢？
B: I have to look at my shopping list. Oh, yes, bread.	我得看看購物單。啊，是麵包。
A: Here's the bakery.	麵包部到了。
B: Please give me a loaf of bread❶ and a box of butter cookies.	請給我一條麵包，一盒牛油曲奇。
C: Here's the bread, fresh out of the oven.	這是麵包，剛剛烘好的。
But I'm afraid we're out of ❷ butter cookies.	可是牛油曲奇給買光了。
How about some coconut cookies?	椰子餅乾怎麼樣？
We're having a special sale of them today.	今天賣特價呢。
B: All right. I'll take two boxes.	好的，我買兩盒。
A: Where to next?	我們跟着到哪兒去呢？
B: To the meat counter.	到肉檯去吧。
A: Ah, here we are.	啊，到了。
B: I want one pound of minced beef and ten slices of boiled ham.	給我一磅碎牛肉（免治牛肉），十片熟火腿。
C: Yes, Sir. Anything else?	好的，先生。還要別的東西嗎？
B: No, thank you.	不要了，謝謝。

B: Now I have to get some canned foods and other groceries.	現在我要買些罐頭食品和雜貨。
A: I think I'd better go and get a shopping trolley for you.	我還是給你找一輛購物車子。
Your basket is getting pretty full.	你的籃子放滿了東西啦。
B: Thanks. Now, let me see. I need two pounds (one kg) of butter, a half pound (a half kg) of margarine, a box of sugar, a small can of table salt and two jars of strawberry jam.	謝謝你。讓我看看。我得買兩磅牛油、半磅人造牛油、一盒糖、一小罐餐桌鹽、兩瓶草莓果醬。
A: I'll help you take the items off the shelves.	我替你把物品從架子上拿下來吧！
Are you particular about the brands?	你有沒有特別喜歡的牌子呢？
B:No, I'm not. Any brand will do.	沒有。甚麼牌子都行。

文法及用法説明

❶ 本課有很多不可數名詞，它們都要加上量詞，以下再舉一些例子：

a pair of spectacles	一副眼鏡
a pair of trousers	一條褲子
a pair of shoes	一雙鞋子
a pair of scissors	一把剪刀
a sheet of paper	一張紙
a piece of land	一塊地
a piece of cloth	一塊布
a sack of rice	一袋米
a bowl of rice	一碗飯
a catty of sugar	一斤糖
a herd of cattle	一群牛

❷ out of在本課中的意思與without（沒有）的意思相同，是一個十分常用的前置詞，例如：out of stock（沒有存貨了），out of breath（喘氣），out of patience（不耐煩）。

Vocabulary and phrases 生詞

2182.mp3

aisles	貨物架與架中間的通道
breads and bakery	麵包與糕點
beverages	飲料
cereal	穀類食物
canned food	罐頭
checkout counter	付款處
condiments	調味醬料
dairy products	奶類食品
frozen food	凍肉
fruit	生果
household items	家居用品
health and beauty	健康及美容用品
meat	肉類
pasta	意大利粉
rice	米類
seafood	海鮮
shopping cart	購物手推車
snacks	零食
wine	酒類
vegetables	蔬菜

19. Home life 家庭生活

2191.mp3

A: Get up, Tom. It's getting late.	湯姆，起來吧，時候不早啦。
B: But it's Sunday today, mother.	媽，今天是星期天嘛。
A: I know, but I want you to sweep the garden.	我知道。不過我想你替我掃掃花園呢。
B: Oh, all right, mother.	好的，媽。

In the bathroom 在浴室

2192.mp3

B: Did you use up all the toothpaste, Mary?	瑪莉，你把牙膏通通用光了嗎？
C: Oh, maybe I did. I'm sorry. Here's a fresh tube.	啊，可能是的，真對不起。給你一支新的。
B: Where have you put my toothbrush and towel, mother?	媽，你把我的牙刷和毛巾放在甚麼地方？
A: Right over there.	就在那邊。

2193.mp3

A: Quickly wash your hands, Tom. Breakfast is ready.	湯姆，趕快洗手。早餐預備好了。
Here's the soap.	肥皂在這兒。
B: I'll have to comb my hair first.	我得先梳梳頭。

2194.mp3

B: What's for breakfast, mother?	媽，早餐有甚麼東西吃呢？

A: Ham and eggs.	火腿蛋。
B: That's wonderful!	真好！
A: Please put some bread in the toaster.	放些麵包到烤麵包器（多士爐）裏去吧。
B: All right.	好的。

2195.mp3

B: Can I have a sandwich, mother?	媽，可以給我一點三文治嗎？
I'm starving.	我餓了。
A: You'd better❶ wait. Supper will be ready soon.	你還是等一下。晚飯很快就做好的。
B: What's for supper tonight?	晚飯有些甚麼菜呢？
A: We're having steak and salad.	有牛排跟沙律。
B: That sounds very good.	聽來很好。

2196.mp3

B: May I turn on❷ the television, Dad?	爸，我可以扭開電視機嗎？
D: Of course. Go straight ahead.	當然可以。你儘管扭開好了。
A: Turn down the volume a bit, Tom.	湯姆，把音量扭小一點。
I think your father wants to read his newspaper.	我想你爸爸希望看看報紙呢。
B: Yes, mother.	好的，媽。

文法及用法說明

❶ You'd better是You had better的縮寫。had形式雖為過去時態，但與better連用時是現在時態，作「不若」或「還是……好」解，後面緊接沒有to的動詞不定式（infinitive without "to"）。had better用於建議或勸告：

You had better mind your own business.	你最好別管閒事。
We had better stay home. It's raining.	下雨了，我們還是留在家裏吧。

❷ turn on的意思為「打開（電燈、收音機等）」：

Please turn the lights on.	請打開電燈。

如果要表示「關掉（電燈、收音機等）」的意思，要用turn off：

Turn off the water.	把水龍頭關掉。

Vocabulary and phrases 生詞

🎧 2197.mp3

television	電視
telly	電視（英式）
channels	頻道
tv series	連續劇集
episode	集
news and weather	新聞天氣報告

soap (soap opera)	戲劇節目（通常受某商戶贊助）
commercial breaks	穿插於節目中的廣告
cookery	飲食節目
documentary	記錄節目
sitcom (situational comedy)	處境喜劇
sports	體育節目
travel	旅遊節目

Exercise 練習

2198.mp3

Answer the following questions. 請回答下列問題。

1. Whose car is it?（their）
2. Whose dog is this?（Mary's）
3. Which dress do you want?（blue）
4. Which bus must I take?（the No.1）
5. Which road should I take?（this）

Answer 答案

1. It's their car.
2. It's Mary's dog.
3. I want the blue one.
4. You must take the No.1 bus.
5. You should take this road.

20. School life 學校生活

2201.mp3

A: John! John! Wait a minute. I want to talk to you.	喂，約翰！等一等，我想跟你談談。
B: Hello, Mary! What's the matter?	喂，瑪麗！甚麼事兒啊？
A: I'm having trouble with my mathematics. Could you help me?	我的數學遇到一些難題，可以幫幫我嗎？
B: I'd be glad to. But Bill is much better at❶ mathematics than I am.	當然可以。不過比爾的數學比我好。
I'll ask him to come along.	我找他一塊兒來教你。
A: Thank you very much. Where shall we meet?	謝謝你啊！我們在哪兒見面好呢？
B: How about the student lounge? It's usually quiet there.	學生休息室好嗎？那兒通常都很安靜。
A: That'll be fine. Our last class is at 3 o'clock.	很好。我們最後一堂課在三點鐘。
Shall we meet at 3:30?	那麼三點半見好不好？
B: I think that'll be all right. But I'll have to check with Bill.	好的，我想沒有問題吧。不過我得問問比爾。
A: All right.	好的。

🎧 2202.mp3

A: Why don't you join our club?	你為甚麼不參加我們的會社？
B: I have no time. I have already joined in many extra-curricular activities.	沒有時間呢。我已經參加了很多的課外活動啦。
A: We meet only once a week❷. Many members play different musical instruments, and sometimes we learn different kinds of folk dances.	我們一個星期聚會一次。一些會員會彈奏樂器啦，有些時候我們則學習各種民間舞蹈。
It's a good chance to meet people and relax.	你可以趁着這個機會認識多些朋友，又可以鬆弛一下。
B: That sounds quite interesting.	聽來很有趣。
All right, I'll go next week.	好的，我下一個星期來吧！

PART 02

文法及用法説明

❶ better為形容詞good的比較級。good at意思為「擅長於……」：

He is good at English.	他的英文很好。
I'm not good at dancing.	我跳舞跳得不好。

要表示對某一方面的東西不擅長，可以用weak in:

He is weak in mathematics.	他不擅長於數學。

❷ once（一次），twice（二次），three times（三次）……表示動作發生的次數，例如： once a day（每日一次），twice a year（每年兩次），three times a week（每星期三次）。

Vocabulary and phrases 生詞

2203.mp3

entrance examination	入學考試
daily schedule (timetable)	上課時間表
extracurricular activities	課外活動
graduation ceremony	畢業典禮
kindergarten	幼稚園
preschool education	學前教育
mid term (examination)	中期考試
primary school	小學
oral-test	口試
quiz	測驗
school discipline	學校紀律
secondary school	中學
teaching staff	教員
tuition fee	學費
university	大學
vocational school	職業訓練學校

Exercise 練習

2204.mp3

Answer the following questions. 請回答下列問題。

1. What did she buy yesterday? (a book)
2. How deep is the river? (fifty feet)
3. What day is it today? (Wednesday)
4. When did you see him? (last week)
5. Where do you come from? (Hong Kong)
6. Which one do you like? (red)
7. Whose pen are you writing with? (her)

PART 02

Answer 答案

1. She bought a book yesterday.
2. It's fifty feet deep.
3. It's Wednesday.
4. I saw him last week.
5. I come from Hong Kong.
6. I like the red one.
7. I'm writing with her pen.

21. Hobbies 興趣嗜好

2211.mp3

A: You have a lot of books here. Do you like reading❶?	你這兒的書好多呀！你喜歡閱讀嗎？
B: Yes. I especially like to read novels.	喜歡。特別是小說。
A: Me, too. I've just got hold of a copy of "Roots".	我也是。我剛剛把一本《根》弄到手呢。
B: Oh, really? I couldn't get one. They were all sold out.	啊，真的？我買不到呢。都賣光了。
A: Yes. I heard that it is one of the best sellers at the moment.	是啊！聽說現在這本書是最暢銷的書之一呢。
B: Have you read it?	你看過了沒有？
A: I am reading it now.	還在看呢。
B: Is it interesting?	好看嗎？
A: Yes, very interesting, and touching, too.	很好看，還十分感人呢。
B: Could you lend it to me❷ when you've finished reading it?	你看完了以後，可以借給我看看嗎？
A: Certainly.	當然可以。
B: What type of books do you read generally besides novels?	除了小說以外，你還看哪一類的書呢？
A: I like to read adventure stories as well as biographies.	我喜歡看一些冒險故事和傳記。
B: I've got several books of these kinds. You can take a look.	我有幾本這類的書，你可以看看。
A: Thank you.	謝謝你。

2212.mp3

A: How do you spend your spare time?	你怎樣打發你的空餘時間呢？
B: I usually go out to take pictures.	我通常去拍照。
A: So you are interested in photography.	那麼你對攝影很有興趣是嗎？
B: Yes, but I'm only a beginner.	是的。不過只是初學罷了。
A: Have you learned how to use any digital imaging software?	有沒有學會用電子圖像處理軟件呢？
B: Yes, I have a Photoshop installed in my computer.	有的。我電腦安裝了相片編輯軟件呢。
A: I am now learning how to edit my photos.	我正在學習怎樣編輯修改我的相片。

2213.mp3

A: You certainly have a wonderful collection of songs.	你收集的歌真是多得很呀！
B: Thank you. I'm crazy about music, so I spend most of my pocket money purchasing and download on the latest songs online through iTunes.	謝謝你。我十分喜歡聽音樂，所以花了很多零用錢在網上購買及下載 iTunes 上最新的歌。
A: Do you like classical music, or do you like jazz and popular music, too?	你喜歡古典音樂嗎？你也愛聽爵士音樂和流行音樂嗎？
B: I like all kinds of music.	各種音樂我都愛聽。

文法及用法說明

❶ reading 為動名詞，其形式與現在分詞相同。動名詞有名詞的作用，亦有動詞的性質，所以稱為動名詞。例如：

Smoking is forbidden in the office.	辦公室內禁止抽煙。
He likes swimming.	他喜歡游泳。

利用動名詞，句子會顯得生動些：

I swam yesterday.	我昨天游泳。
I went swimming yesterday.	我昨天去游泳。

❷ lend...to... 為借東西給某人的意思，而 borrow...from... 則是向人家借東西：

I lent a book to him. (I lent him a book.)	我借了一本書給他。
He borrowed a book from me.	他向我借了一本書。

Vocabulary and phrases 生詞

2214.mp3

bird watching	觀鳥
doing gardening	弄園藝
listening to pop-music	聽流行音樂
going for movies	看電影
swimming	去游泳
playing jigsaw puzzles	玩拼圖
practicing martial arts	練武術
playing football	踢足球
playing snooker	玩桌球
playing chess	下棋
reading books	看書
working on a computer	玩電腦
roller-skating	玩滾軸溜冰
photo-taking	攝影
watching tv	看電視

22. Sports 運動

🎧 2221.mp3

A: I like cycling myself.	我喜歡騎自行車。
B: Me, too. It's good for ❶ health.	我也喜歡。這運動對身體很有益處。
A: What other sports do you like besides cycling?	除了騎自行車以外，你還喜歡甚麼運動？
B: I enjoy hiking and swimming. Both of them are fun. And they help me keep fit. I usually go swimming every week.	我喜歡遠足和游泳。這兩種運動很有樂趣，又可以使我身心健康。我每星期都去游泳。
A: Oh? Where do you go? I'd like to join you some weekend.	啊？你去哪兒游泳呢？找一個週末，我跟你一塊兒去。
B: That'd be fine. I generally go to Victoria Park.	很好。我通常到維多利亞公園去。
They have a good swimming pool there.	那兒有一個很好的游泳池。
A: And where do you go hiking?	那麼你去哪兒遠足呢？
B: Usually in the New Territories. But I prefer to go hiking in the autumn. The weather's too hot now.	通常到新界去。我還是喜歡秋天時去遠足，現在天氣太熱了。

🎧 2222.mp3

A: I know that football is very popular sport in Hong Kong.	踢足球在香港是十分普遍的運動。
But what about other sports?	其他的運動又怎麼樣呢？
B: Well, basketball and volleyball are very popular.	籃球跟排球也很普遍。

Many people like to play tennis, table-tennis and badminton, too.	很多人也喜歡玩網球、乒乓球和羽毛球。
A: Are the courts and playgrounds very crowded?	球場和遊樂場都很擁擠嗎？
B: Yes, especially during the holidays. You have to book the courts beforehand.	是啊！尤其是假期的時候。我們通常都要預先定好地方。
You know, there is a lack of❷ space for recreational activities here.	你知道嗎？我們這裏十分缺乏遊戲的地方呢。
A: Oh, I see. No wonder I saw so many children playing all sorts of games in the streets the other day.	原來如此。怪不得那天我看見很多小孩子在街上玩着各式各樣的遊戲啦。

2223.mp3

A: I enjoy ice-skating very much.	我很喜歡溜冰。
B: I've never tried ice-skating. Is it difficult?	我從來沒有試過溜冰。溜冰難學嗎？
A: Not especially. Once you've learned how to keep your balance, the rest is easy.	不太難，只要知道怎樣去平衡身體，其他的都很容易啦。
B: Then you'll have to teach me. I'd like to learn.	那麼你得教教我了，我希望學會溜冰呢。
A: I'll be happy to. Oh, it's time to leave for the match.	十分樂意。噢，我們該去看球賽啦。
I don't want to be late.	我不希望遲到。

B: Neither do I❸. This is the first time I've been to a stadium to watch a ball game.	我也不想。這是我第一次到球場去看球賽。
I usually watch them on TV.	通常我都是看電視台播映的比賽。

文法及用法説明

❶ Good for在這裏解作「有益的」：

Exercise is good for the health.	運動對身體有益。
Fresh air is good for you.	新鮮空氣對你有益處。

❷ a lack of為「缺乏、缺少」的意思，lack為名詞。lack又可以用作動詞：

He is lacking in courage.	他缺乏勇氣。
He lacks experience in handling such matters.	處理這類事件，他缺乏經驗。

❸ 同意別人的説法，而句子是否定的話，就不能用So do I等一類的語句，而要用Neither do I.例如：

I don't like it.	我不喜歡這個。
Neither do I.	我也是。
I'm not hungry.	我不餓。
Neither am I.	我也是。

Vocabulary and phrases 生詞

2224.mp3

cycling	單車（自行車）
diving	跳水
fencing	劍擊
gymnastics	體操
referee	裁判
springboard diving	彈板跳水
wind surfing	滑浪風帆
swimming	游泳
backstroke	背泳
breaststroke	蛙式
butterfly stroke	蝶式
free style	自由式
badminton	羽毛球
shuttlecock	羽毛球所用的球
baseball	棒球
basketball	籃球
billiards	英式桌球
cricket	板球

golf	高爾夫球
hockey	曲棍球
ice hockey	冰上曲棍球
table tennis (ping pong)	乒乓球
volleyball	排球
water polo	水上排球

23. Entertainment 娛樂

2231.mp3

A: Are you free this evening?	今天晚上有空嗎？
B: Yes.	有空。
A: I've got two tickets for a concert, and I thought you'd like to go.	我有兩張音樂會的票子。我想你會喜歡去的。
B: I'd love to. What concert is it?	當然喜歡去啦。是甚麼音樂會？
A: The National Orchestra is specially invited❶ to play in the concert.	他們特地邀請了國家交響樂團給音樂會演奏。
You will hear some of the famous works of Beethoven.	你將會聽到貝多芬一些著名的作品。
B: Oh, that's wonderful. What time shall we meet?	啊，好極了！甚麼時候見？
A: 7:30 at the City Hall. All right?	七點半在大會堂，行嗎？
B: All right. See you then.	行。再見。
A: See you.	再見。

2232.mp3

A: I'd like two seats in the back stalls for the 7:30 show.	給我兩張後座的票子，七點半那一場的。
B: I'm sorry. The tickets are sold out.	對不起，票子賣光了。
A: How about the dress circle?	那麼超等呢？
B: There are no tickets left there, either.	超等也沒有票子啦。

A: Let's book seats in advance for the 7:30 show tomorrow.	不如我們預定明天七點半的票子吧。
C: All right.	好的。

2233.mp3

A: What's on❷ TV now?	電視在上演甚麼節目呢？
B: There's Western movie on Channel One.	第一台上演一部西部片子。
A: How about Channel Two?	那麼第二台呢？
B: It is showing a variety show.	正在上演一個綜藝節目。
A: And Channel Three?	那麼第三台呢？
B: It has an educational program on.	正在上演一個教育節目。
What would you like to see?	你喜歡看甚麼呢？
A: I'd like to see the Western.	我想看看那部西部片子。

文法及用法説明

❶ is invited 為被動語態（passive voice）的形式。被動語態表示主語是動作的承受者，其結構為助詞be加上動詞的過去分詞（past participle）。下面每組句子的第一句為主動語態（active voice），第二句為被動語態：

He writes a letter.	A letter is written by him.	他寫信。
He wrote a letter yesterday.	A letter was written by him yesterday.	他昨天寫了一封信。

He is writing a letter.	A letter is being written by him.	他正在寫信。
He has written a letter.	A letter has been written by him.	他剛剛寫了一封信。
He will write a letter.	A letter will be written by him.	他將會寫信。

PART 02

❷ 這裏的 on 作「上演」解：

What's on at the Ocean Theatre? 海運戲院上演甚麼片子？

Vocabulary and phrases 生詞

2234.mp3

cinema	電影院
action	動作片
adventure	歷險故事片
animation	動畫片
biography	傳記片
comedy	喜劇
documentary	紀錄片
drama	劇情片
horror	恐怖片
romance	愛情片
musical	音樂片
science fiction	科幻片
thriller	驚慄片

war	戰爭片
western	西部牛仔片

2235.mp3

dance	舞蹈
ballet	芭蕾舞
waltz	華爾茲舞曲

2236.mp3

concert	音樂會
classical music	古典音樂
concerto	協奏曲
duet	二重奏/唱
matinee	日場
opera	歌劇
solo	獨奏/唱
quartet	四重奏/唱
quintet	五重奏/唱
sonata	奏鳴曲
symphony	交響樂
symphony orchestra	交響樂團
trio	三重奏/唱
theatre	劇院

24. Asking the way 問路

2241.mp3

A: Excuse me❶, but could you please direct me to the railway station?	對不起，請給我指示一下到火車站去的路程好嗎？
B: I think you've come the wrong way.	我想你走錯了路啦。
A: I always get confused in this area.	我在這一區常常迷路的。
B: You just walk straight on and turn right at the second corner.	你向前行，然後在第二個街角向右轉。
A: I'm very much obliged to you.	真感激你啦。
B: Not at all.	不用客氣。

2242.mp3

A: Excuse me. How do I get to the City Hall?	對不起。怎樣走才到大會堂呢？
Do I take this road or that one?	該走這條路還是那一條路？
B: Take this road.	走這一條路吧。
A: Is it far from here?	離這裏很遠嗎？
B: Yes, it's quite a distance.	是啊！路程頗遠呢。
A: Can I get there in ten minutes?	十分鐘可以到嗎？
B: It'll take longer than that. I should say thirty minutes' walk❷.	不只十分鐘呢。我看差不多要走三十分鐘。
A: Is that so? Then maybe I should take a taxi. Thank you very much.	真的嗎？那麼我還是坐計程車好啦。謝謝你。
B: You're welcome.	不用客氣。

2243.mp3

A: I'm sorry to trouble you, but is there a police station near here?	對不起，麻煩你了。這兒附近有沒有警察局呢？
B: Yes. You go to the other side of the road through this pedestrian subway. Turn the corner and you will see the police station.	有的。你穿過這條行人隧道，到了對面。然後轉一個街角，就可以見到警察局了。
A: Thanks.	謝謝你。

文法及用法説明

❶ 向別人問路，要先説Excuse me或Pardon me，然後才提出詢問，例如要問到郵局去的路，可以這樣説：

Excuse me, but can you tell (show) me the way to the post office?

Excuse me, but can you tell me where the post office is?

Excuse me. Does this road go to the post office?

Excuse me. Which of these roads goes to the post office?

❷ thirty minutes' walk解作「走三十分鐘的路程」：

The park is ten minutes' walk from my house. 公園離我家要走十分鐘的路程。

Vocabulary and phrases 生詞

2244.mp3

Go straight on.	一直往前走。
I'm a bit lost.	我有點迷路了。
Is it far to walk?	步行路遠嗎？
Should I take a bus?	我是否應該坐公共汽車？
Is the MTR station far from here?	地鐵站離這兒遠嗎？
Which way is the station, please?	請問車站是走哪條路？
I'm not sure. I'm just passing through.	我不太清楚，我只是路過。
It's no distance at all.	一點兒不遠。
It's just round the corner.	就在街角處。
It's just across the street.	就在街對面。
You can't miss it.	你不會找不到的。
Yes, it's that way.	好的，在那邊。

Exercise 練習

2245.mp3

Listen to the following conversations and answer the questions that follow. 請聽以下對話，然後回答對話後面的問題。

A stranger is asking the way. 一個陌生人正在問路。

Questions:

1. What is the stranger trying to find?
2. Is it far away?
3. Which does she take, a taxi or a bus?
4. Where is the bus-stop?
5. Where must she get off?

Answer 答案

Stranger-S   Passer-by-P

S: Excuse me. I'm trying to find the National Hospital.

P: Oh, it's quite a distance. You'd better take a taxi or bus.

S: I think I'll take a bus. Where's the bus-stop?

P: There's one in front of the post-office. You must get off at the third stop.

S: Thank you very much.

1. The National Hospital.
2. Yes, it is.
3. a bus.
4. It's in front of the post office.
5. At the third stop.

25. Traffic 交通

2251.mp3

A: Hey, taxi!	喂，的士！
B: Where to, sir?	先生，到哪裏去呀？
A: To the Ocean Centre, please.	請載我到海洋中心去。
B: Yes, sir.	好的，先生。
A: Can we get there in fifteen minutes?	十五分鐘可以到嗎？
I'm in a hurry to keep an appointment.	我趕着赴一個約會呢。
B: I'm not sure, sir. There seems to be a lot of traffic today.	我不知道哇，先生。今天的交通好像很繁忙。
I hope we won't get into a traffic jam.	希望不會遇上塞車吧。
Anyway, I'll try my best.	不管怎麼樣，我盡力而為啦。

2252.mp3

A: When does the next train to Tai Po leave?	下一班往大埔的火車幾點鐘開呢？
B: At 11:30, sir.	十一點三十分，先生。
A: I'd like 2 round-trip tickets❶ to Tai Po, please.	請給我兩張到大埔去的來回票。
B: Here you are, sir.	好，先生，這是你的車票。

🎧 2253.mp3

A: From which platform does the train leave?	火車從哪個月台開出呢？
B: Platform number two.	第二號月台。
A: Thank you.	謝謝你。

🎧 2254.mp3

A: I want to go to Waterloo Road. Which way should I go?	我想去窩打老道，該走哪一條路呢？
B: You may either go by ferry or❷ by tunnel bus.	你可以坐渡海小輪，又可以坐過隧道的公共汽車。
A: I think I'll go by tunnel bus. Which number should I take?	我坐隧道公共汽車吧。該坐哪一條路線的車呢？
B: You'd better take number 103.	你最好坐第103號線。

文法及用法説明

❶ 乘搭火車時，有兩種票子，一種為單程票（single ticket），另一種為來回票（round-trip ticket 或 return ticket, 美國則叫 two-way ticket）。

❷ either...or 為連接詞，有以下的用法：

Either you or he is wrong.	或是你錯，或是他錯。
You may take either an apple or an orange.	你可以拿一個蘋果或者一個橙子。
Please either come in or go out.	請你或是進來，或是出去。

either...or 指兩者選擇其一，而 neither...nor 則指「既不……也不……」：

Neither you nor I could go. 你和我都不能去。

Vocabulary and phrases 生詞

PART 02

2255.mp3

bus	巴士（公共汽車）
double-decker	雙層巴士
cross- harbour tunnel	紅磡海底隧道
eastern harbour crossing	東區海底隧道
western harbour crossing	西區海底隧道
mass transit railway	地下鐵（香港鐵路）
octopus card	八達通卡（智能卡付款系統）
public light bus (minibus)	小巴（公共小型巴士）
peak tram	山頂纜車
ferry	渡海小輪
tram	電車
taxi	的士（計程車）
fares	車費、船費

Exercise 練習

2256.mp3

Listen to the following conversations and answer the questions that follow. 請聽以下對話，然後回答對話後面的問題。

Lily and Mary get into a taxi. They arrive at the station. Lily pays the driver, and they get out. The following dialogue takes place at the station. 莉莉跟瑪麗坐上一部計程車，抵達火車站。莉莉給計程車司機付了車費後，他們便下車了。下面是瑪麗跟莉莉在火車站的對話。

Questions:

1. Who are going to the station?
2. What time does the train leave?
3. What time does Lily make it?
4. What is the correct time?

Answer 答案

Mary-M Lily-L

M: Hurry up, Lily. It's 6:25, and the train leaves in 10 minutes.

L: I am hurrying, but your watch is fast. I make it 6:20.

M: No, it is 6:25. Take a look at the station clock.

L: Oh, yes. I guess you are right. Well, I must go and get our tickets,then we can get on the train.

M: All right.

1. Lily and Mary
2. 6:35
3. 6:20
4. 6:25

26. Welcoming someone 歡迎

2261.mp3

A: Mr. Smith, I presume❶?	我想你是史密斯先生吧？
B: Yes, I'm William Smith from Chicago.	是的，我就是威廉・史密斯，從芝加哥來的。
A: Welcome to Hong Kong, Mr. Smith. My name is Wu.	史密斯先生，歡迎你到香港來。我姓胡。
B: I'm very pleased to meet you, Mrs. Wu.	胡太太，很高興認識你。
A: I have a letter of introduction to you from the president of my company.	這是我公司董事長給你的介紹信。
B: It was very nice of you to come and meet me.	你來這兒接我真好啊。
A: It's nothing at all. And how was your flight across the Pacific?	不用客氣。你坐飛機橫渡太平洋，旅途愉快嗎？
B: It was perfectly delightful. Thank you.	十分愉快，謝謝你。

2262.mp3

A: Welcome back to Hong Kong. Did you have a good time in Europe?	歡迎你回到香港來。在歐洲玩得開心嗎？
B: Yes, I enjoyed the trip very much.	很開心，我的旅程十分愉快。
A: You must be very tired. I have a car waiting outside.	你一定很累了。我有車子在外面等着。
Come this way, please.	請這邊走吧。

B: Thank you.	謝謝你。
A: Are these bags yours?	這些提袋是你的嗎？
B: Yes.	是我的。
A: Do you have any other luggage❷?	還有沒有行李？
B: No, just these two bags.	沒有啦，只有這兩個提袋。
A: Let me carry them for you.	讓我替你拿吧。
B: Please don't bother. I'm sure I can manage.	不要麻煩了，我自己來。
A: Well, at least let me carry one of them.	那麼讓我拿一個吧。
B: All right, if you insist❸. Thank you very much.	要是你堅持的話，就給你拿一個吧。謝謝你啊。

文法及用法說明

❶ presume的意思為「推測、假定」，與take it that...的意思大致相同：

I take it that we are to come early. 我以為我們該早來。

❷ luggage（行李）與baggage意思相同；baggage為美語。

❸ insist為「堅持」的意思：

He insisted on (upon) his own ideas. 他堅持自己的想法。

She insisted on (upon) the importance of being punctual. 她強調守時的重要。

27. Seeing someone off 送別

2271.mp3

A: Well, here comes my train. We'd better say good-bye here.	啊，火車來了。就在這兒分手吧！
B: Have a good summer, John.	約翰，祝你過一個愉快的夏天。
A: Thanks, thanks for coming out here to see me off.	謝謝你，謝謝你來這兒給我送行。
B: Not at all. Drop me a line❶, will you?	哪兒的話。寫信給我好嗎？
A: Sure. I'll write as soon as I get there.	好的。我一到那兒就寫信給你。
B: Well, so long.	那麼，再見吧。
A: So long.	再見。

2272.mp3

A: Thanks for the party last night. I had a great time.	謝謝你昨晚開的晚會，我玩得很開心呢。
B: Not at all. It's a pity that you're leaving so soon.	哪兒的話。你這麼快就走了，真可惜。
A: I must thank you again for your warm hospitality.	我得再三謝謝你熱情的招待。
A: I've really felt at home❷.	我真有賓至如歸的感覺呢。
B: The pleasure's mine.	這是我應該做的。
A: They are making the final call for the flight.	我的班機作最後召集呢。
A: I'm afraid I must go now. Please give my regards to your sister.	我看我該走了。請替我問候你的姊姊。
B: Thank you, I will. Have a nice trip!	好的，謝謝你。一路平安！

文法及用法説明

❶ to drop somebody a few lines（給某人寫信），to drop somebody a postcard（給某人寫一張明信片）。

❷ be at home, to make oneself at home, to feel at home都解作「無拘束」，好像在自己家中一樣。

Exercise 練習

🎧 2273.mp3

Answer the following questions. 請回答下列問題。

1. When will he leave Hong Kong?（on Friday）
2. When does the train leave?（at four o'clock）
3. When will she come back?（next month）
4. When did he tell you the bad news?（a week ago）
5. When will they get married?（on 1st of May）

Answer 答案

1. He will leave Hong Kong on Friday.
2. It leaves at four o'clock.
3. She will come back next month.
4. He told me a week ago.
5. They will get married on 1st of May.

28. At the airport 在飛機場

2281.mp3

At the Airport 在飛機場

A: Where's the Cathy Airline. check in❶ counter?	國泰航空公司的行李檢查處在哪兒？
B: Over there.	在那邊。

2282.mp3

At the counter 在檢查處

A: I'm taking Flight CX707 to New York.	我是乘CX707班機到紐約去的。
C: Please let me see your ticket and passport, madam.	請讓我看一看你的飛機票和護照。
A: Here they are.	這就是。
C: Please weigh your luggage.	現在請你把行李過磅吧！
A: Do I weigh all my luggage?	所有行李都要過磅嗎？
C: Yes, except your hand-luggage.	是的，除了你的手提行李之外，都要過磅。
A: Is it over weight?	會不會超重呀？
C: No, madam, just below the limit.	不會的。
C: Here's your boarding pass. Thank you.	這是你的登機證，謝謝你。

2283.mp3

Before flying-off 起飛前

A: It's very kind of you to see me off.	你還親自來送行，太客氣了。
D: It's nothing. I hope you have enjoyed your time in Hong Kong.	沒有甚麼。這些日子你在香港玩得好嗎？
A: Of course. I've enjoyed every moment.	好，玩得很好。
D: How many hours does it take❷ from here to New York?	從這兒到紐約要飛幾個小時呀？
A: I think it will take about 17 hours.	大概要十七個小時吧！
D: Please come and see us again.	有空請你再回來。
A: Yes, I will. Thank you very much.	一定回來，謝謝你。
A: I shall be very glad if you will come to New York.	我也歡迎你到紐約去。
D: Thank you.	謝謝你。
A: I think I must go now, good-bye!	我該告辭了，再見！
D: I hope you will have a pleasant trip home. Good-bye!	祝你一路平安，再見！

文法及用法說明

❶ check in 的意思為到達某一處地方，例如機場、旅館、工廠等，並且辦理登記手續。如果付了賬離開（例如在旅館），則叫做 check out。

❷ take 在這裏的意思為「需要」、「必要」，例如：

The work took six hours.	這項工作花了六小時。
It takes five people to play the game.	玩這個遊戲需要五個人。
It takes four minutes to go to the bank.	到銀行去要四分鐘時間。

Vocabulary and phrases 生詞

2284.mp3

airline	航空公司
arrival	到境
departure	離境
flights	飛機航班
boarding card	登機證
luggage	行李
hand-carried luggage (baggage)	手提行李
overweight	過重（行李）
travel insurance	旅遊保險

non-stop flight	直航飛機
delayed	誤點（延誤）
take-off	（飛機）起飛
land	（飛機）降落
business class	商務客位
economy class	經濟客位
passport	護照
safety belt	安全帶
fasten your safety belt	繫緊安全帶
window seats	靠窗口的座位
aisle seats	靠走廊的座位